LINN B. HALTON

I live in a small village in Gloucestershire with the man I fell in love with, virtually at first sight. We were at a party and our eyes met across a crowded room! My days are spent with characters who become friends and Mr Tiggs, a feline with catitude. I always knew that one day I would write romantic novels, but I never dreamed they would have a psychic twist! I've experienced many 'unexplainable' things, but it took a long time for me to accept the reality of what that means. Love, life and beyond…but it's ALWAYS about the romance!

Forever

LINN B. HALTON

Harper impulse

HarperImpulse an imprint of
HarperCollins*Publishers* Ltd
77–85 Fulham Palace Road
Hammersmith, London W6 8JB

www.harpercollins.co.uk

A Paperback Original 2014

First published in Great Britain in ebook format by HarperImpulse 2014

A catalogue record for this book is
available from the British Library

ISBN: 9780007591640

This novel is entirely a work of fiction.
The names, characters and incidents portrayed in it are
the work of the author's imagination. Any resemblance to
actual persons, living or dead, events or localities is
entirely coincidental.

Automatically produced by Atomik ePublisher from Easypress

I would like to thank Kim, Heidi, Kate, JB, Erin, Susan, Shaz, Charlotte, Dizzy C, Nikki and Tobi for valued feedback throughout the writing of this series and amazing support - love you guys! Also Mandy and Janice - for being a listening ear and for constant support and guidance.

To my friends and colleagues at Loveahappyending Lifestyle emagazine - writers who share their knowledge and from whom I've learnt so much!

To all of the HarperImpulse team - for your energy, enthusiasm and the buzz you create that writers and readers are loving so much!

Lastly I have to thank 'my rock', Lawrence, without you by my side I wouldn't be able to devote all of my time to writing...

Prologue

Ceri isn't meant to fall in love, as she is here for one purpose only. Alex is supposed to cross her path briefly and give her the confidence to move on and fulfil her destiny. It's meant to be a turning point for them both – but in opposite directions.

Ethan Morris, a well-respected medium, gave Alex a warning after receiving a message for him from the other side. Ceri receives her own warning when it's made very plain to her that she is responsible for her own actions and will have to put right anything she changes in error. Alex begs Ceri to meet with Ethan, but she refuses to believe what he has to say and manages to convince Alex that he could be wrong. Psychic medium Mark Kessler becomes Ceri's spiritual mentor. Her confidence begins to grow as she gains an awareness of her work on both planes of existence, something that can only be granted to an angel.

As Ceri and Alex cling to their relationship things begin to unravel and, at their engagement party, Alex's past catches up with him. At the same time Ceri faces the stark reality that fate cannot be cheated…

Alex

Chapter One – You Can't Run From The Truth

"She's gone, Ethan. Ceri's disappeared and I think it's because of Alicia." There's silence on the other end of the phone and I can't stop myself from pacing back and forth. "Are you there? Hey man, I really need your help."

Ethan lets out a sigh. "Alex, I tried to warn you. You can't mess with fate and I know you both felt you were meant to be together, but clearly this is telling you something. You lulled yourselves into a false sense of security. Call it wishful thinking. I don't know what else I can say to you." He sounds grim.

"No, this is different. Honestly, this isn't about our being together, it's about the abortion that Alicia had. If only I'd told Ceri everything at the very start... I'm a complete and utter fool!"

"How did she find out? I'm rather surprised it should come to light after all these years. What were you, eighteen or something when it happened?"

"Yeah and I know it's a long time ago, but my parents recognised Alicia at the engagement party. I think Ceri put two and two together, and then suddenly she was gone. When I went back to the flat some of her things were missing, but there was no note, as if she had been spirited away." My voice cracks and I grit my

3

teeth, trying to stop myself from shaking.

"I think you are forgetting one thing," Ethan's tone is forceful.

"What?"

"Ceri is an angel. She would be able to connect with Alicia's emotions on a much deeper level. Nothing can remain hidden, unless she has a close and personal involvement with the other person."

"How could I forget—man, I've blown it!"

Ceri

Chapter Two – Facing Facts

The split second I bumped into Alicia it was as if the inside of my head had exploded. I saw the energy of a baby and felt the love. That bond between mother and child. It was only meant to briefly experience the wonders of those early weeks of growing, safe inside the shell of someone with whom she will forever be linked. Out of all of the zillions of energies, we each have a 'family' in tune with our own unique vibration who are with us forever. No matter what happens, or which plane we are on, that bond never weakens. That's why the power of love is so strong and miracles sometimes happen, fuelled by an emotion that can transcend everything.

I knew instantly that I had to leave the party, to walk away from Alex before he had the chance to officially place that ring on my finger. It would link us with a promise that I couldn't make, simply because I knew it was wrong. My heart was in pieces, but my ethereal mentor was calling me and directing me to leave.

It was an impossible situation and at first I seriously doubted I had the strength of character in this mortal body to obey. As I pushed clothes into the holdall and gathered the things that I would need I knew that I wasn't just leaving Alex, but also Seb. It was unfair on my dear brother who, despite the sad memories, had come home to help celebrate our engagement.

But I wasn't running away. This wasn't something of my choosing.

"Why?" I asked the voice with no name, as our minds linked and his thoughts filled my head.

"Because it was never a part of the plan for your earthly life, Ceri. I think you knew the moment you touched Alicia that she is the next person you have to help. In order for Alicia to heal and forgive herself for the decision she made about that young soul, she needs to hear Alex say he understands. That will bring them together once more, because that is their true destiny."

"No!" The sound that came forth was hardly recognisable as my voice. "I can't give him up. I can't survive here without him. Please, I'm begging you." As fast as my feet were taking me away from the apartment, a part of me was hoping I would soon be making my way back. "Please don't wrench us apart."

"I'm not the creator. It isn't in my power to change anything and you know that's not how it works. No one questions the path, it's simply there and in each life it's different. Alicia has suffered for many years and it's now time for the suffering to end. Destiny is a part of creation, everything evolves through experiencing emotions and when Alicia returns to spirit she will be able to help others along their path. She will have empathy and understanding that can only come from experiencing something first-hand. You are destined to understand the loss of true love. There is no turning back, Ceri. As an angel you know that."

His words spoke the truth, but my human form was much frailer than my spirit energy and one was overpowering the other.

"Pull yourself together. You have important work to do. You will have to work at sorting out the situation you have made so much worse than it need have been." The tone of his voice was more of a reprimand than his words. I know I created this mess. If I had listened to my instincts, or even the guidance I'd been given, Alex and I would simply be good friends. Alicia coming back into his life would not have been a problem. I hung my head in shame. There is no such thing as a fallen angel… or is this yet another earthly anomaly?

Chapter Three – A Message For Me

I knew each step towards building my new life was going to be mercilessly straightforward. I would have welcomed a battle, if only to have an excuse to let rip the horrible mix of emotion within me. The path mapped out before me is clear. The plan was merely to disconnect myself from Alex completely, so that he would realise it was over between us. Alicia is his future, but it's too soon for him to understand that. The circumstances have yet to unfold.

I threw my SIM card away and purchased a new number as soon as I'd found a place to rent. It was on the other side of town, so there was little likelihood of bumping into Alex and it meant I could still keep my day job. It is all happening so instinctively, now I'm really listening to what my core vibes are telling me, that I hardly have to tune in. This isn't about starting over again, only correcting one painful mistake: sleeping with Alex, oh, and falling in love with him.

I try to accept the inevitable, simply because I – of all people – should know better. Alex's pain wears more heavily upon me than my own. He emails me dozens of times each day.

I will never stop loving you until my last breath...

I need you, I can breathe without you. I can't sleep, I can't eat...

I know you would not do this to us unless you had no choice...

I forgive you, but I cannot believe in a divine power who would think of our love as anything other than something extraordinary and meaningful. I go on because I'm too cowardly to take the easy way out...

I lie in bed at night and my hands remember your body, my mouth longs to kiss you just one more time...

Nothing matters to me now, without you by my side. I will accept it because I know how much you love me. You can't hide that from me. We belong to each other no matter what...

There has to be something we can do, Ceri, I can't accept this. I don't care if I go to hell, if that's the price I have to pay...

His emails are long, his mood swings reflect the emotional rollercoaster he's on, one moment desperate and the next forgiving. Each one tears another hole in what's left of my heart.

If only Alex could understand there is no heaven or hell, no price to pay as such. But if I hadn't walked away I would have robbed him of a future that has already been mapped out for him. Imagine the repercussions as this one major change ripples outwards, affecting future generations. There is no hell Alex, my soul cries out to him silently, only the whole of creation and the universe. This life is just a tiny part of that.

But I've come to understand something else. Something that I don't think even my ethereal mentor can see. And that is the fact that this life counts for everything when you are here. Alex is a much younger soul than I am, so our paths might never touch again on any plane. The tears I shed might as well be blood. Each little droplet represents a part of me that is dying, once lost, never to be regained – on either plane.

I mark Alex's emails as spam so they no longer drop into my inbox. I cannot delete them, read or unread, and change the setting to never auto delete. I don't know why, because all is lost and there is no turning back. It's not that I fear being punished, it doesn't work in that way. No one checks the work we do. It's all instinctive and the emotions that bring out the worst in humans – jealousy, anger, hatred – simply don't exist other than here. Everyone works quite happily for the good of the universe and with joyous intent; it's really so simple I can now see it's almost laughable. Earth life is like a film full of special effects and when the film is over everyone goes home to reality.

My new reality is cold and stark. It is a life without Alex.

***

Weeks have passed and each day has been a struggle for my human persona, although my spiritual self is progressing in leaps and bounds. So much so that Mark has admitted I've outgrown his mentoring.

"You're a strange one, Ceri. I've never had a student like you before. At the start I realised you had a very intuitive sensitivity, but within such a short space of time I can't believe how you've developed. Things that took me a long time to adjust to, and skills that required honing to a fine degree, seem to come so naturally to you. There's nothing left I can offer. You have outgrown your teacher." He sounded in awe and also a little sad.

"You helped me find myself Mark, and for that I will be eternally grateful. You taught me to stop fighting my instincts and listen to the inner me. I feel like I've been reborn." I reached out and touched his arm, giving it a gentle squeeze. I wanted this man to know I was indebted to him. I still felt guilty that I couldn't explain how exactly my eyes had been opened and that I live my conscious life on two very different planes. He understands that we all visit the ethereal world when we are in a deep sleep, but in this life he will not have knowledge about how angels work. It's so frustrating, as he has his suspicions, although his theory isn't quite correct.

That's what scared me so much when Alex went to see Ethan. Ethan is a more highly evolved being and he knows exactly how angels work. That's why he told Alex we were not meant to be together. He could see the path stretching out before me, even though I seemed intent on changing it.

"It will be strange not having you there when I'm on stage. I've enjoyed calling you up and you must be delighted with the reception you've received. You must stretch your wings now and confirm the bookings you've been offered. People warm to you instantly when you are on stage receiving messages. I think a large part of that is down to the way you so easily tap into the emotions coming through. I'm so proud to have been a part of your development, it's been a privilege." Mark isn't usually an overly emotional man, but tonight he's opening up the most sensitive part of himself.

"Thanks, that means so much to me! Now, go and meditate. Clear your head, because you're on in fifteen minutes."

We exchange smiles and part. Mark heads off to the quiet room and I walk back into the hall to sit in the audience.

He has a great session. His messages are clear and well received by all. There's hardly any negativity amongst the audience, which is unusual. Fortunately, the vast majority of people who attend an open evening with a psychic medium come hoping for a message from a loved one. Each will be seeking something in particular, whether its confirmation their loved one has safely passed to the other side or forgiveness for something they regret. A handful will be there merely to prove to themselves it's fake.

People don't realise that the message in itself is not important, because in spirit nothing that happens on earth is of any consequence. It's a training ground, where we learn about right and wrong, hope and disappointment. Emotions make the soul grow, and some of the awful things that happen here on this earthly plane happen only for the reason of allowing a soul to grow and gain understanding. Humans have the power of free choice and it's the same in spirit. No one controls us, but then again there is no need. Earth is the only plane where bad things exist.

Free will was given so that people could experience having to make choices. On the ethereal plane that isn't an issue, we are all simply involved in fostering harmony and spiritual growth. But a part of our job is also to support those on the earth plane, as it certainly isn't an easy existence. For those energies that come back repeatedly to help others on their path, each life can be very different. No life is entirely easy, but some are incredibly hard and that level of experience is always a sign of a more evolved soul. The extreme experiences are reserved for those who can utilise and share their learning, upon their return. My ethereal mentor once told me that being in the presence of someone even closer to the centre of creation than him was a truly humbling moment. His words were "the purity brought tears to my eyes".

A round of applause fills the room and it takes me a moment or two before I realise one of the other guys on the stage is pointing directly at me. As the hall falls silent I feel the colour rising in my cheeks. The man walks down the steps at the side of the stage and approaches me from the centre aisle.

"I'm sorry." He apologises as he walks towards me, eyes firmly locked on mine. "I have one more message and this man isn't going to let me go until I've delivered it. Are you happy to accept it?" He seems concerned and I know he will expect me to answer; we all want verbal confirmation from the recipient as we never like to offend.

"Of course." My voice sounds a little uneven. I'm nervous to be on the receiving end.

"He says that there is no looking back. That you have done well, but you must not weaken. He keeps repeating that because it's important." He's silent but holds up a hand to me, as if to say 'wait'. "Let go, he's saying, but I'm not sure what that refers to.

And, oh, there's some validation. You recently returned something – it was in a small box. He's touching his heart with his hand. I think this means that it was a really important moment. Like a turning point in your life. That's all I have, he's withdrawing. Thank you for listening."

I nod my head and say a quiet thank you. He walks back to the stage, hardly aware of the power or meaning of his message. I glance across at Mark, who stands up to address the audience and say a final goodnight. He indicates for me to join him as he descends the steps.

"Are you okay?" He places his hands on my shoulders. I see an instant reaction: he senses something but says nothing.

"I'm fine, really," I try to reassure him. I'm still shocked at having received a message in an open forum. It seems someone is intent on making sure I don't fall back on my commitment and that I stay focussed on the task ahead. My heart constricts and I have to swallow the lump that suddenly appears in my throat. My outward appearance might seem calm, but my heart is crying out to the universe. Forgive me, I meant no harm... don't let Alex suffer because of me.

Chapter Four – Moving On

"Seb, it's me."

"Ceri, where are you? Alex is demented with worry. Why did you disappear and what's wrong with your phone?" He sounds worried and a little angry.

It's understandable, and I feel guilty that he's still in the UK. I know he had only planned a short stay and the fact he's still here means he wouldn't leave until he knew I was safe. But there was no way I could make contact any earlier. I had to organise things and allow enough time to pass, so that it would be very clear to Alex that I'm not going back to him.

"I've found a place to rent. It's a long story Seb, but I'm safe and well. I can't be with Alex anymore and you must encourage him to move on and accept that. I'm so, so sorry for what I've done and the way Alex is hurting, I know it's entirely my fault. I'm really glad you're still here, because he needs you. Thank you."

Seb lets out a loud sigh. "Ceri, we called the police, but fortunately someone saw you only a couple of miles away and rang us. They were travelling on a bus and by the time it stopped and they went back to find you, you were gone. If it wasn't for that sighting, the police would be dragging the river and your photo would be plastered everywhere. What were you thinking? How irresponsible!"

As he vents his anger I know all I can do is listen. He's right, but then he doesn't know the situation I'm in. There was no choice in it for me and that sighting was divine intervention. Everything happens for a reason – and I have to stifle a laugh. So many people say that phrase. Few understand what it really means.

"Look, I'm sorry and I'm fine. You didn't fly back—" I can't hide the guilt that echoes in my words.

"Are you kidding me? My twin sister goes missing from her own engagement party. I've heard of cold feet, but this is insane. Alex is a great guy, Sis, and you've hurt him in the worst possible way. You owe him an explanation at the very least. What's gotten into you all of a sudden? You're supposed to be the sensitive one! I know he should have told you about his past, but he was very young and he made a mistake. It was a long time ago and I'm sure he would have told you in his own time. Since when did you become so unforgiving? This makes no sense to me at all."

He finally runs out of steam and I let a moment or two pass without answering.

"Believe me, Seb, if I could turn back the hands of time, I would. Alex and I should have remained friends and no more. I can't really explain, but I wanted something that I wasn't meant to have and now I have to make amends. Alex needs to find someone... less complicated. Please don't repeat any of this to him, just say we've spoken. Tell him I'm safe, but that it was a mistake, and if he really loves me he will understand when I say that it could never work for us. It's better we split up sooner rather than later. We have to accept that and move on. Seb, I need you to do this for me and it's vital you convince him I'm serious. It's important, and you are the one who can do this for me." I think the begging tone in my voice is enough to convince him.

"I thought I'd lost you too..." His anger has dissipated and he's referring to losing his precious Anna. My heart bleeds for his loss and the pain that I can feel, despite the distance between us. But he's healing, albeit slowly, and I wonder if having to support Alex during the last few weeks has been cathartic for him. Maybe it took his mind off his own problems for a short while.

"Look, I'll text you my current address, but only on condition you don't give it to anyone. The same goes for my new number. I'm going to ring Sheena next."

"Now I feel awful. I've quizzed Sheena because I couldn't believe she wasn't in on it. I thought she was hiding what she knew about your whereabouts. You really are okay, aren't you? Should I be worried about anything?"

"I can't pretend this hasn't knocked me for six. This is so not what I wanted to happen, but sometimes we're not in control of our own destiny. Alex must be convinced that this is what I want, or he won't move on. I can't allow him to suffer that way, so please, be the friend he needs at this moment in his life."

"Okay. I'll do what you ask on the condition that you pick up whenever I ring and you agree to meeting up with me soon. I want to check out for myself where you're staying. There's going to be a lot to sort out as Alex's apartment is let for another two months."

"He can stay there as long as he wants, tell him that. I would like some more of my clothes though and I'm going to ask Sheena to call in and pack them up for me. Do you mind being the one to break the news to Alex? It's not fair that I ask Sheena, but I also feel it will be easier for Alex if it comes from you."

Seb lets out another long sigh. I can tell that he thinks I'm making a big mistake, but what can I say? If I told him the truth he would probably call in a psychiatrist.

"You're breaking Alex's heart, and treating him this way is out of character, Ceri. I thought you would understand. A young, naive couple made a mistake and having an abortion has scarred Alicia for life. Alex didn't have a say in it and I understand that doesn't matter, it takes two to make that sort of mistake. But did you stop to think about the reason *why* he didn't tell you about it in the first place? It changed him, and has affected every relationship he's had since. This isn't simply old baggage, it's an old

18

wound that has never healed."

This is a sensitive side of Seb that I haven't seen before, he's almost pleading on behalf of Alex. It sounds like Alex has poured his heart out to Seb and yes, I knew from the start that Alex carried some old wounds, but I had no idea what had happened. Seb doesn't understand that this isn't about Alex's past, but his future. I can't explain that, so I have to cut short this conversation before I let something slip.

"What's done is done. I'm sorry if it seems cruel, but I have Alex's best interests at heart."

"I never thought I'd ever describe you as cold, Ceri. I think you seriously need to examine why you are doing this, for your own sake, as well as Alex's. Don't forget, I want to meet up with you soon. I'll tell Alex, although what exactly I'm going to say, I don't know."

He disconnects abruptly, before I can say anything else and I lean back against the wall, my eyes closed as my whole body begins to shake. Is it possible to cry without tears? My body is crying out in agony over the unfairness of this situation, for the love I have for Alex that will never die.

"I love you Alex and I always will. If we can't be together in this life, then I'll do whatever I have to do to ensure we are together in the ethereal world. I don't want to be an angel if it means I lose you forever."

The room around me is silent.

***

It took me two days to recover enough to call Sheena.

"Oh my poor Ceri!" Her sympathy was tangible the moment she heard my voice. "Seb called and said you were fine, that he couldn't tell me anything else other than you would be in touch. I can't tell you how many times I've checked my phone each day. Are you safe? What do you need?"

The part of me that I've struggled to hold together begins to unravel as her concern touches my core. Sheena has known me for so many years and even in the midst of this mess, when the whole world will think I'm being cruel to Alex, she's worried about me.

"It's horrible. I want to curl up and die. Everything's such a mess and it's entirely my fault. I couldn't face anyone, even though I knew you would all be worried. Seb is so angry with me and I know I've broken Alex's heart. He's paying the price for my selfishness but please, believe me when I say I'm doing this for him." I can't stop the tears escaping, and trying to keep myself from outright sobbing is difficult. I'm an empty shell, hollow inside where there used to be love and happiness. I can sense that Sheena understands the enormity of my situation and that there is more to it than I can convey.

"My dear girl, whatever has happened is complicated. I know you well enough to understand that. You wouldn't walk away from the man you love unless you had a good reason, and I know it's nothing to do with Alex's past. He believes that you hate him for his part in what happened, but it's the psychic thing interfering, isn't it? Look, I know how accurate your instincts have been in the past, so do what you have to do. I'm here to help pick up the pieces. Whatever I can do to help, you only have to say, and Seb is being a tower of strength in supporting Alex."

"I don't deserve your kindness. I've done something very wrong accepting Alex's love and it's his future that I'm fighting to protect. Why did I think I knew best? Better than the advice I'd been given... free will is a bad thing. It can mess everything up."

"Ceri, I don't understand. You aren't making much sense. Look, I'm going away tomorrow for three weeks, but when I get back we'll spend some time together. If you need me I'm only a phone call away. You won't do anything silly, will you?"

A moment passes as a memory flashes through my mind. "No. You don't have to worry on that score. My life isn't my own."

Sheena exhales slowly. I've failed to reassure her, but what else can I say without breaking even more of the rules?

I've been told that I will live this earthly life for another fifty-two years. While death is a welcoming thought, it isn't in my fate and I know that willpower alone can't overturn what has been decided. I thought I could change things, make it happen because it felt so right but, as the saying goes, pride comes before a fall.

Chapter Five – A New Normality

My reputation as a psychic and medium is growing. It's largely due to Mark spreading the word. All of the venues where I accompanied him have offered me slots in their annual programme. I'm also beginning to receive bookings for one-to-one sessions and although the thought terrified me at first, I haven't had a difficult one yet. I was concerned I might find myself sitting across the table from a client and my mind would be blank – no messages, no vibes – and what would I do then? Say "sorry, there are no messages for you" and send them home? I'd voiced my fears to Mark, thinking he might laugh, but his answer demonstrated my fears were only natural.

"That's not a problem you are going to have to worry about, Ceri. Some people go out there before they are ready, or with such a big ego that they don't listen as carefully as they should to their spirit guides. It's teamwork channelling messages, and there's no 'I' in team."

His confidence in my abilities was rather difficult to handle. I didn't have the same level of optimism. Then, suddenly, here I am – doing what I'm supposed to do and every step forward is so easy, I can't make a wrong move. Even I'm surprised by some of the things that I hear myself saying. How do I know all of this? From time to time my work on the ethereal plane is more difficult and demands my conscious time. That's the only way I can explain it. Some days I'm hardly aware, unless I sit and meditate and then I'm there, on the other plane and living it. When it's a difficult problem I'm dealing with, it can overlap with my consciousness here and I feel like I'm actively living two lives at the same time. Two sets of thoughts at the forefront of my mind competing for attention. A repeat of what happened that first morning after I talked Alex into believing we could have a relationship. I was here, but I knew I was also somewhere else at the same time. Even worse, I chose to totally ignore everything that Ethan had said in the message for Alex, as if it didn't count.

What worries me now is that I can't avoid Ethan forever. He's a working psychic medium on the same circuit and our paths will cross at some point. What will I say? "Sorry I snubbed you, when I knew everything you had told Alex was correct. I thought I could change what fate had in store for us"? I knowingly tried to sow seeds of doubt in Alex's mind about a man whose abilities far outweigh Mark's and I feel ashamed of myself. I had the worst motive for trying to discredit his words. I wanted Alex to love me without reservation.

In the ethereal world there is only good intention, and there is no ego or need for self-preservation. Energies don't put themselves first, because it isn't necessary. But the earthly part of me feels very real at times and I was fighting for something so precious it was almost heart-stopping. I wanted Alex's love in this life, more than I respected the laws of the universe. Why? This earthly life is harsh, cold and cruel at times, and yet it's also full of emotions that can overwhelm the senses. The suffering some individuals have to bear seems extreme and tortuous. Why have such an intense training ground? Maybe the centre of all being is admitting that creation and the ongoing perpetuity of the universe is missing something? The power created by emotions that can be all-consuming, that can make a weak person strong, and it doesn't exist anywhere other than here. I now understand that I am a splinter, a part of

23

the spark of life that is creation. It lies within us all, of course, but some sparks are instrumental. Few angels experience an earthly life because our powers do not require that input: we are highly evolved, but are we emotionally evolved?

So here I am, alone, with my heart torn to shreds. Alex is no longer a part of my life and I have no choice but to accept that with grace and humility. It was my transgression that caused the pain both Alex and I have to endure, and the weight of that lies heavily upon me. The load is lightened every single time I pass on a message for someone whose life will be altered by what they hear. Sometimes it's very sad: in this world where there are atrocities that are hard to stomach there is also a wonderful sense of nurturing, compassion and sacrifice. Tonight I saw a woman who had nursed her mother through her final months of life. She was totally unaware that her mother was around her all the time and will be until the day she dies. They are kindred energies from the same family, and will be together throughout all of time.

While the message was positive and very personal, those on the ethereal plane are not allowed to share detail about their non-earthly existence. Therefore the messages are mainly validation, to give comfort, or guidance when someone is in danger of losing their way. The woman who came to me was looking for forgiveness. Towards the end of her mother's life she was required to make some tough decisions about her care, and the guilt she was feeling was overwhelming. In truth, the answer should have been that it didn't matter when her mother was here, and it most certainly doesn't matter now. Her mother's energy is back working on the ethereal plane and helping lower energies, and even humans, achieve their full potential. But her eye will always be on her daughter, because they are one and the same and always will be. For those energies that have experienced at least one earthly life, I can now understand the level of compassion they feel. I know my life here will never be the same now that I've known, and lost, my beloved Alex. I will never get over having to walk away from his love. Am I destined to be the first angel to harbour regret? The thought scares me beyond belief, because that reflects the human side of my nature only. I fear it means my ethereal energy is now damaged. Is that what is referred to here as a fallen angel? If that is the case, I have fallen into the depths of earthly hell and if it was within my power I would end my life here and now. The truth is that life without Alex isn't worth living.

It's strange that in the depths of misery the sun still shines and the birds still sing. Nature continues to surprise and delight, whether that's a glorious blue sky or heavy rain sweeping across barren fields. There is beauty everywhere and in everything, if you take a moment to notice what's happening around you. Now I spend my days showing others how to see with open eyes and passing on messages that are positive, meant to bring comfort or direction. However, what is important isn't the fact that it often helps to make their grief more bearable, but that it's a step towards their spiritual awakening. It strikes me that those who care the most, suffer the most. Earth logic is so hard to understand at times.

Chapter Six – Pain

I thought I had felt pain... and then I linked with Alicia. The pain of losing the man I love is nothing compared with the pain in Alicia's life. That fateful decision is the first thought in her head each morning as she awakens and the last thought on her mind at night. She isn't in love with Niall: she tries hard to convince herself she is, because he has shown her such kindness. He recognised in her a need to be protected and he does that with love and devotion. She is everything to him and the fact that he is unable to father a child and give her what he feels she longs for eats away at him. Everything he has achieved pales into insignificance, when the one thing he really wants in life is beyond his grasp.

They are together in their unhappiness and that is their common bond. Ironically, if they had succeeded in having a child, I feel that the differences between them would have divided them over time. Irrespective of that, their fate does not steer them along the same path. Niall cannot help being business-focussed and that trait will never change. Alicia knows that happiness and material goods do not bring happiness. It's almost too much for one human to bear and it's clear to me when I visit her, that she cannot continue like this for much longer. Something is going to break and that's why this task has been given to me.

Alicia has strayed off her life path because she can no longer identify with her inner voice, which is pitifully full of self-loathing. She stays with Niall because he clings to her and that isn't good for either of them. He deserves to be with a woman who can love him just as deeply in return. The fact that Alex has been determined as Alicia's soul mate is testing me beyond belief. I am an angel, but a part of me is human while I'm here doing my work and it's that part I struggle to control. Feelings of jealousy and resentment are new, alien emotions that are much stronger than I could have thought possible. I have to keep zoning out the human pull on my nature and concentrate on the task in hand.

My heart bleeds for her pain and real sense of loss. She's a practical woman in many ways. She understands that regretting her decision doesn't mean that having made a different one would have been the right answer. She's not spiritual and doesn't practice a religion, but there is a seed of belief within her. She finds herself having conversations with "whatever is out there" and it's the way she's managed to keep sane, despite the pressures. She has only paid lip-service to the years of therapy she's undergone, aware that the healing comes from within. But the stumbling block is always that inability to forgive herself.

What hurts me most is that I can now see so very clearly that Alex too has suffered. He has carried this around with him for a long time, unable to admit how he feels to anyone, even me. His share of the guilt is as real as Alicia's and it made him the man he has become. Subsequent relationships never lasted very long, because after the abortion he felt inadequate. He had failed to inspire a belief in his ability to be a provider and make a commitment, which he feels is the reason Alicia made her decision without consulting him. Suddenly everything falls into place, and the fact that he fell in love with me is even more incredible.

I've been told I have the strength to complete my tasks, I hope that's true. At the time I had no idea at all how deeply my personal beliefs and emotions would be tested. The worst is yet to come and I know I cannot fail.

"Seb." I wrap my arms around him and we hug each other with a sense of sadness. The last time we embraced was supposed to have been an occasion of celebration and joy, but it ended so abruptly when I had to leave the party.

His own pain is still visible in his aura, his daily fight to keep on an even course continues. One slip and he risks losing his grasp on the new life he is beginning to build. That is the greatest fear he has ever had to face, greater than the mountains he has climbed or the heights he has scaled. It breaks my heart, and I know that an angel's life on this plane is never going to be an easy one.

"You look tired," he admonishes. He stands back and scrutinises my face. "And you've lost weight."

I stand aside to let him enter and his eyes flick around the tiny entrance hall. I wonder if he thinks I've left Alex for someone else and he's looking for subtle clues.

"Coffee?"

"Yes, thanks."

Seb follows me through into the tiny kitchen. "How long are you renting for?"

"Three months, it's someone I know at work. It's going on the market once the painters have been in to freshen it up. They're moving in together..."

"What a mess." Seb takes a seat at the bistro table.

"How's Alex?" I can't help myself asking the question.

"In pieces. He hasn't been to work since the day you left and he's talking about handing in his notice. He's in no shape to even pretend his life is normal and I'm encouraging him to think about freelancing. It will be less pressure if he can work from home, and doesn't have to face the world if he doesn't feel up to it." He grimaces and I understand how bad it must be.

"He will get over this. There is someone out there for him. It just isn't me."

28

"Well, we all have to trust your judgement on that one. You broke his heart not once, but twice." His tone is clipped, he thinks I'm wrong and he doesn't approve.

"I know I'm not the one for him and I bitterly regret that fact. Believe me, if I could change this I would." A tear trickles down the side of my face and I turn away.

I stir the coffees and carry them across, sitting down next to him. "I've missed you so much and I'm sorry you were dragged back, only to have more grief. Thank you for stepping up and being strong for Alex. I don't know what would have happened if you hadn't been here." I reach out and place my hand on his arm. Our eyes lock for a brief moment.

"I figure I owe you, Sis. You've always been there for me." His voice is softer, emotional. "Is there any way at all you can see yourself getting back together with Alex? This isn't just cold feet or something?"

"No, Seb. I tried fighting my destiny and look how many people have ended up getting hurt. Free will is a dangerous thing and I'm being taught a difficult lesson. If Alex can get through this, there is a bright future ahead for him. Much happiness and love."

Seb absentmindedly moves his coffee mug around the table.

"I'll do what I can. I'm flying out again next week, but I'll be checking in with Alex every day in case he needs to talk. He's a very private guy, we both are really. I've listened to him baring his soul about his past and his feelings for you, and in return he's listened to my problems. It's been cathartic in a way and it takes someone in the depths of their own sorrow to understand another person's pain."

"I'm proud of you, Seb. Your silver lining is there, I promise you."

"But is there happiness for you?" His eyes reflect his concern for me. His frown is like a question mark. He's asking me if I can see my own future, but the answer is no.

"Lots of things bring happiness. Sometimes getting what we think we want doesn't make things right. What's that saying? Be careful what you wish for, it might just come true." I laugh with the irony. "I can't grab my happiness at the expense of someone else. It goes against everything I believe."

"That's why I'm an atheist." Seb says bitterly. If I believed his words I would be horrified, but I can see what's happening inside him and it's an awakening. "Do you need anything?"

"I'll survive. I always do."

Chapter Seven – Learning To Forgive

Working with Alicia is tiring. Thankfully my day job is going well and I'll be moving back into my own apartment very soon. I received an email from Seb to tell me he'd found himself a salaried job with an aid agency. Then followed the words I had been dreading. Alex moved out a few days ago and Seb told me Alex had posted the keys back through the letterbox. Our final link was severed, but I was too numb to react.

It's strange to be working on so many different levels at the same time. I'm being given guidance and support which has allowed me to stand back and assess things with a new clarity. I hadn't mentioned anything to Seb, but Alex leaving Grey's is a part of the next step towards growing closer to Alicia. The relationship between herself and Niall is floundering. Not because he has any suspicions about what happened in the past, but because one-sided love doesn't work. She cares for him and idolises him in many ways, but the spark isn't there. Niall is beginning to realise that and he will let her go.

I focus mainly on sending her positive and healing thoughts. Connecting with her mind and making each step forward clear and concise. That is bolstering her self-esteem and she is beginning to listen to her inner self again. She can make good decisions and she can move on. We are both benefitting and the connection we have is helping to heal me. The raw emotions after my split with Alex are beginning to heal over, as I accept my earthly fate. Ironically Alex has had a hand in that, although not quite in the way I think he meant.

Shortly after Seb flew out, Alex contacted Ethan again. He asked him to talk to me. Alex doesn't have my telephone number, but he knew Ethan would be able to find me. The psychic network is a close group and avoiding Ethan hasn't been easy for me, but he sought me out.

"Ceri, it's been a while."

I was thrown when I heard his voice and turned around to see he was holding out his hand. We shook and his handshake was firm. I was taken aback by his aura. Why had I thought he was judgmental when I met him before? He's an old soul and I cringe, thinking that the last time we met things were very different. I hadn't been called back at that point and I only had my intuitive understanding. My angel work was not a part of my consciousness. Seeing him now I feel guilty for the way I dismissed his advice and tried to talk Alex into questioning his theory. He knew the truth: that no good would come of trying to enforce what we both wanted over what fate would allow.

"Ethan, I didn't know you were here tonight." I feel awkward, but I know he will understand the change in me and hopefully forgive the way I acted.

"I'm not here working. I heard you were going to be here so I thought I'd pop in and see how you were doing. Could we meet up afterwards for a drink?"

He's being very casual and it would be rude of me to refuse, but I know Alex has asked him to come.

"Okay. I'll meet you at the wine bar in the High Street, about nine-thirty?"

"Great, hope you have a good session." He flashes me an encouraging smile.

"I hope so too."

It was a great night and it reminded me that my angel work is essential. So many messages, so much hope to foster and corrections to make that will allow the true course of destiny to follow through. Granting free will to those who have lost touch with their inner wisdom has been damaging. I'm sure there are those who wonder why the creator doesn't make sweeping changes and over-ride a decision that seems dubious.

It doesn't quite work like that. Take fate, for example. All of the little things I correct have to be done subtly, or the ripples caused will actually do even more damage. Once a change has happened, it impacts on other things. Managing it isn't straightforward. The only recourse at a higher level would be to dispense with the earth plane entirely, and it does serve a valuable purpose. I really believe that it is required to keep everything in balance by teaching valuable lessons. I once jokingly thought there was an inherent design flaw, and I could feel my ethereal mentor's disapproval. What made me think I could ever grasp the whole concept of being? I felt humbled and determined to work even harder to fulfil my part in the process. But now I've lived the theory and I have a story to tell that is stranger than any fairytale.

It means something to me that I have the power to make a real difference to people's lives. I know I have to come to terms with losing Alex's love and let go of the resentment I often feel. Even anger has coursed through my veins, in the early hours when I lie awake wanting him, needing him. He must hate me now and maybe that's not such a bad thing. It doesn't stop my heart from aching and my body from missing his touch, but at least he will no longer harbour hope. Hope, I've come to learn, can be a soul destroying emotion.

As I find myself walking towards Ethan, I wonder just how much he understands about me. I suspect it is much more than anyone else I know.

"Ceri, that was great!" He pulls out a chair for me to sit next to him at a small corner table. "I didn't order drinks as I wasn't sure what you might want."

"A glass of white Grenache would be lovely, thank you."

He disappears and returns a few minutes later. He's carrying one large wine glass, a pint of local ale, and a selection of things stuffed into his two jacket pockets. I give a nervous laugh.

"What?" He shrugs his shoulders, puzzled at my reaction. Placing the glasses on the table he empties his pockets, like a magician pulling rabbits from a hat.

"How did you know I was going to be hungry?" I ask, still stifling laughter.

"I always am after a session – all that nervous energy. Big changes for you, I see." He settles himself down, slipping off his jacket. I sit back and study him for a moment. What can he sense? When Alex initially introduced me to Ethan, I didn't take to him at all. With hindsight, was that down to the fact that he was trying to tell me something I didn't want to believe?

"What do you mean, getting up on the platform? I've been doing it for a couple of months now and each time is a little easier than the one before. I've surprised myself and yes, I suppose you could say some things have changed quite significantly."

He lays out the snacks in front of me. "Ladies first."

I pick up a packet of crisps and give him a grateful smile. I guess we have a few things in common, and maybe he isn't as condescending or judgmental as I first thought.

"Thanks." I give him my best polite smile. "What did you want to talk about?" I watch his face and his reaction is a mix of emotions. He feels awkward and he raises his beer glass to his mouth, taking a generous slug.

"We both know why I'm here, and I told Alex I didn't think it was a good idea. I've been thinking about our first meeting, Ceri, and feeling rather guilty. I didn't handle it very well, which is unusual for me. I'm used to giving bad news and I should have realised how shocked you were going to be. I misread the signs."

I stop munching and look at him intently. "What signs? Are you saying your theory was wrong?" I hold my breath, although I know full well he was right. But hope leaps in my heart to think there is even a slight possibility.

"No, sorry, I can't change what I said. The message was very clear. I simply mean you are a different person now. I don't know what's happened but your aura is amazing. The Ceri I was talking to then probably couldn't grasp the concept of warnings via a dream. Something has been awakened in you. I feel you can read me like a book. The tables have turned. I'm astounded."

I have to be careful what I say. Even though Ethan's vibration is a wonderful thing to behold, he isn't an angel. I have no idea if he's ever met one before, although I doubt it.

"I had a good teacher, and this is my path. I understand now and all I want is for Alex to be happy. I want him to find the person he's destined to spend the rest of his life with. I really wish I was the one, but I'm not. I'm also sorry I took my disappointment out on you. It was nothing personal."

"I know. No explanation necessary, let's call it quits. It reminded me that I can never make assumptions, even when I sense someone is spiritually enlightened."

We sit looking at each other for a few moments. He's a very tall guy, although he's rather self-conscious about that. I like that he's a straight talker and he isn't glib. I can now see why I felt uncomfortable around him, because the truth is all I did was challenge everything he said. I feel embarrassed, despite the way he's trying to smooth over the awkwardness.

"What will you say to Alex?"

Ethan raises his eyebrows in a sad way. "It will sound like more bad news I suppose. There's no point in giving him false hope. I'll be gentle though, and I don't think he really expected anything to come of this chat. Mainly he wanted some reassurance that you are okay. He loves you so much it's still his first concern."

"Life can be very cruel sometimes, you understand that more than most. I can't hide how this has torn me apart, but it's the right thing to do. The only thing."

It's weird, but psychics rarely talk about the messages they receive and pass on. Mostly that's because we have to open up to be receptive. It's like preparing to meditate. There is a process of opening up the chakras so that the spirit world can connect. Afterwards there is a similar closing down process. When in a receptive state, the channel is wide open, but once we finish our work it is indeed the same for anyone else – we leave it all behind us. The personal stuff we pass on isn't ours to mull over or contemplate, we are simply the spokesperson. We are the medium that handles the communication process. Often, after a session, there is little I can remember and at first I found that very strange. I wonder what Ethan remembers. Obviously enough to know there's no point in giving Alex any hope.

He downs half his pint and sits back. "There was a lot of negativity in that room tonight," he reflects.

I nod. "It still terrifies me every time I stand there. I wonder if my mind will go blank and nothing will come."

"Smart lady." He smiles. "Never take anything for granted. No one ever said it was going to be an easy line of work and there are times I know a message will be wasted. It falls on deaf ears. I'm relieved you've found your niche though, and that you can accept what's coming. It's time to move on."

"It will become easier, but some days it's still tough. Alex has a friend, Alicia, has he ever mentioned her?"

"Ah, you know..." He pretends to be distracted, as someone squeezes past his chair.

"He told you the story. He's such a sensitive guy, and it's only recently I've come to appreciate the link between his past and the way he perceives himself. He still feels he failed in some way and I'm hoping that together they can move forward. Be instrumental in healing each other..."A meaningful glance passes between us.

"Understood." His tone is accepting. "I'll do what I can."

"Thanks. I'm so relieved Alex has you to talk to, Ethan. I know how busy you are."

"I don't mind being busy, although the travel gets me down sometimes." He's beginning to warm to me and I'm pleased about that.

"Can't make home life very easy."

"Well, after a very messy split a couple of years back, I can vouch for the fact that working evenings and weekends isn't conducive to keeping a partner happy."

"Oh, I'm sorry. I didn't know."

"It's fine, I'm over it, and I'm not always the easiest person to live with. Jess wasn't a believer and as time went on that came between us. When the question 'how was your day?' crops up, it isn't easy to answer when you are sitting opposite someone who wishes you would go out and find a proper job."

I burst out laughing. "She didn't say that, really, did she?"

"Yep, after fifteen years of studying and honing my craft, count-less interviews, talk shows, twelve published books and a busy schedule, every single argument came back to the same thing.

"The lesson I learnt was humility. It's easy to be fooled by all the praise and the positive feedback. But never forget that this is something we are given as a blessing and that it isn't something of our own making."

The more I hear, the more I'm liking this guy. He's a little rough around the edges compared to Alex. Nothing about him is sleek: he looks a little worn. He's the sort of guy who might dress in the morning and forget to look in the mirror to check his appearance. I bet he hates formal interviews.

"Some lessons are best learnt the hard way," I mutter.

"Amen to that."

Chapter Eight – Picking Up The Pieces

As the months pass I'm increasingly caught up with my psychic work and travelling further and further afield to attend events. I can foresee a point when the day job will have to go, as even working three days a week is becoming a juggling act.

With no significant other in my life, and my new friends being mainly mediums I tour with, I've had to find a hobby. It was Ethan who suggested it would be cathartic for me to write a journal looking back over what has happened. He told me the idea had been "given to him" and that means someone in spirit put forward the suggestion. He indicated that there might be another reason that people out there would connect with what I was saying. He also talked about spiritually-inspired writing. It wasn't something I was familiar with, so he lent me half a dozen booklets written by a medium from the US. It was a series of discussions with various angels and I was surprised by the level of accuracy. There were inconsistencies, but I wondered if that was purely misunderstanding, poor communication, or intention. Some things are not meant to be known and fully understood in this life. If I had read any of this prior to my eyes being opened to my spiritual life, I would have sought out this man. His words were astounding and clearly he wasn't merely talking from personal knowledge, but from detailed interaction with the spirit world. Ethan said if

I was interested in spiritually-inspired writing, he could help me tune into the process. It wasn't something many on this earth were offered and he said I should feel flattered.

He's actually a very nice man. Well, nice sounds rather bland, as he can be quite forceful at times because of his beliefs, and he can be impatient. Initially I mistook that as being judgmental, but I can now see it's often because he's frustrated by people's reactions. He genuinely wants to help when he can see someone struggling. If the messages he receives fall on deaf ears, he takes it as a personal knock. I can see why his partner thought he was difficult to live with at times, especially if she didn't share his passion. He lives for his work and is so focused he often forgets to eat. He works too hard and over-commits in his attempts to reach out to anyone who comes forward. Often his diary is full of meetings and sessions with little thought given to him having some down time to relax.

A part of that is an occupational hazard I suppose, and I'm beginning to be affected in much the same way. Even my normal day job doesn't really help me to establish a separate life away from spiritual things. When you work part-time, people are used to you being there less frequently. They often forget to invite you to some of the social after-work sessions. I'm glad about that at the moment. It's really hard not to feel depressed about the fact that the only person I will ever truly love is Alex. It sort of defeats the purpose of even thinking about relationships. There's a guy, Tom, who keeps asking me out, and I've told him straight I don't date toy boys. He laughs, but I am serious. He's five years younger than I am. It isn't solely that, it's also because there's no spark and there never will be. If I said yes because I'm lonely at times, that wouldn't be fair on him.

Sheena flits in and out of my life according to her work schedule and keeps hinting that it's a shame Ethan is alone. I know Madame Voleta said I wouldn't be alone forever, but she didn't qualify that in any way. I don't know if angels who visit earth can have a normal, human life. Perhaps that's because it would be too much of a distraction. Our role is not to be a part of creating future generations, only to correct the things that go wrong.

When Sheena came across my journal, she made me tell her all about it. That was an awkward moment, as she only knows a small part of what has happened. For some reason I felt that there would be no harm in telling her a little more. I never mentioned the word angel but I explained that my life had an agenda and she assumed I was talking about destiny.

Well, that's sort of what it's all about, so I didn't bother to enlighten her any further. At least now she has some understanding of the reason behind my behaviour.

"Don't you feel that maybe you and Ethan have been thrown together for a reason?" she said one day, when we were walking home from the cinema.

"No, why?"

"Well, you weren't very complimentary about him when Alex first dragged you to his office, and after that I felt you were simply looking to pick a fight with him."

I laughed. "Oh, really? It was a case of not agreeing with what he had to say and he was a little abrupt. Not the best start."

"Do me a favour and give him a chance."

I looked at her suspiciously. "Don't try to match-make, Sheena. Anyway, I'm not sure I'm his type."

Sheena smiled, and then tried to hide it. "I'm not suggesting you marry the poor guy, he knows your reputation. I'm simply saying that a relationship can be many things and sometimes companionship and shared interests are a good base upon which to build a friendship. He could be your BSB, no strings attached." She raises her eyebrows.

"What the heck is a BSB?" I'm clueless.

"Best sex buddy – some put it a little more bluntly, of course! Wake up girl, are you in the real world or not?"

"Is that what happens with the singles set now? I'm not sure I approve," I admit, rather shocked.

"Oh come on, if some of us had to wait for Mr Right to appear there would be a chance we'd never, ever have sex. It isn't like a mindless one night stand with someone you don't know. It avoids that horrible moment when you wake up next to someone and find yourself wishing you were anywhere other than in bed with a virtual stranger. I'm talking nice, comfort sex between two mutually consenting adults. Someone you can trust, who is in the same position as you are, waiting to see if their soul mate is around the next corner. Someone who can help take away that feeling of loneliness on a mutual basis."

"Sounds rather pathetic to me," I mumble. I'm mortified that my best friend has been thinking about my sex life.

"I know your situation is a bit different, Ceri, but what if it's the same for Ethan? If you are both going to end up lonely workaholics on a mission, why not see if there's a deeper friendship lurking underneath? Having a BSB stops you making a mistake because you're—"

I hold up my hand. "Stop right there! I don't need you to organise my personal life, even if you think you have my best interests at heart. I can sort whatever needs sorting and I'm not that desperate. Really." I feel myself colouring.

"Sex with Ethan is out of the question, then?" She looks concerned and I feel guilty. My response sounded rather snappy.

"Why are you suddenly so intent on getting me to jump into bed with someone?"

She looks at me, guiltily, as if she's hiding something.

"Because Alex has been sleeping with Alicia for a little while now, I think. He's moving on and I don't feel that's the case for you. Not deep down inside. You're stuck and afraid to let go of that last little thread."

I shut my eyes and bow my head, trying to quell the pain that stabs at my insides. I have achieved my task, they are getting back together and the healing guidance has not been wasted. All of the hours I spent watching Alicia and sending her positive little thoughts, gradually rebuilding her self-esteem to enable her to feel whole again. I haven't opened any of Alex's emails, which have continued to fill up the spam box on my laptop. Stupid, I know, not to have emptied it and even to have withdrawn the automatic monthly deletion. I check it regularly, half hoping they will continue to appear and yet knowing I should be hoping they will stop. I can't read his words – for both our sakes. I have no link whatsoever to Alex, other than the dreams I have, which are more like a fantasy playing out in my head. While my spiritual side carries out the work I have to do, the dream-like state before and after deep sleep is obsessed with the need to be with him. It's enough to keep me going, but I'm ashamed of the way I can't let go. It's the only piece of me that is totally mine, a time when no one in spirit can enter my thoughts. Even my ethereal mentor cannot link with my mind when I'm in that sleepy state – neither fully awake, nor in a deep sleep. It's the private part of my mind where I can imagine a wonderful life of doing good things, but with Alex by my side.

"Ceri, I'm sorry. I shouldn't have told you. Are you going to be okay?" I open my eyes and Sheena looks fraught with concern.

"I'm fine. I'm glad that Alex and Alicia have found each other again, that's good for them both. I was... thinking about Ethan. Maybe you are right, but if anything happens it will have to be initiated by him. Then I'll take it one step at a time."

Sheena leans across and puts her arms around me. "Now I've found my Mr Right, I want you to find some happiness too," she murmurs.

"I know you mean well, but maybe I'm not ready yet to move forward. And I have my work, which I love."

"You were the one who always used to warn me that being married to your work isn't good for you." She laughs, raising one eyebrow in amusement. "I admit I've wasted years on the romantic front, but that was my fate. Now I have Sam, I know he's the one."

Her words fade to a whisper and I can see that she feels guilty talking about her happiness at a time when I'm in limbo.

"There are only so many times you can be a bridesmaid before eventually it's your turn. Sam is perfect for you and he was worth the wait."

"Yes," her voice can't hide the depth of her feeling. "He was worth the wait."

"Can I ask you one thing?" I hate to pose this question, but I need to know.

"Fire away." She sounds hesitant, despite her words.

"Is Alex in love with Alicia?"

"Oh, Ceri, my darling girl. I suspected as much. He isn't lost to you, is he? Would you sacrifice your spiritual work to be with him, if it wasn't too late?"

"That isn't a choice I can make. If it was that simple, the answer is yes, I would. But you misunderstand me. I want him to be happy, I'm just not sure he knows what he wants after what I put him through. Is he clinging to Alicia because it appeases his conscience for what she's suffered all these years? Or has he rediscovered whatever they had?"

She stirs her coffee absentmindedly, deep in thought. "I can only pass on information that has come my way. It's not as if Alex confides in me, but he maintains contact. It's been like that ever since I sent him that email after he upset you – that seems like a distant memory now. It's always brief, asking how I am, and he never mentions you but I know he's hoping your name will crop up. He said that he didn't want me hearing it from anyone else and that Alicia has left Niall. She's staying with him, although he said it was only for a short while. I think he was being diplomatic and I assume he wanted me to let you know. Maybe he thinks it will jolt you into action and make you realise that sometimes you have to listen to your heart."

"I wish you could understand, Sheena, I really do. You have to live my life to grasp how little control I actually have over everything that happens. Sometimes I feel like a passenger on a train that's heading for a crash and there's no way I can halt it. I'm frightened and alone, but still the train thunders on. My heart wants you to say that he doesn't love her, he's simply looking after her. My head tells me that I want him to find peace, love and contentment. I know Alicia is capable of that, and more, if she can find the right person."

"I don't know, Ceri. I just don't know, and that's the truth."

***

It was one of those days when it rains endlessly and you find yourself stuck indoors because there's no real reason to venture out. A part of you is glad about that, but it begins to feel as if you are cut off from the world. I lean my head against the window pane and watch the rivulets of water cascade down, hitting the window sill with force and spraying outwards. The grey day reflects my mood. I've just had a session with Alicia and she's doing so well I can scarcely believe it. I am glad for her as the tension leaves her body, and even her migraine attacks are now under control. She is blossoming and a part of that, I'm sure, is down to Alex. The irony of the situation is not lost on me.

Sheena is in Germany at the moment and life is quiet. It's the slow season in the run up to Christmas and so there are fewer psychic fairs and evening audiences. My one-to-one sessions are still very busy. It's all about personal recommendation and my name is being passed around. A lot of the sessions are happy ones, positive messages for people who only need pointers to keep them on the right path. Now that my work with Alicia is less intensive, I feel something is missing. My ethereal work ticks over in the background and seldom bothers me.

The phone rings and I drag myself back into reality.

"Hello?"

"Ceri, it's Ethan. How are you?"

I haven't seen him for two weeks. He's been up in Scotland attending a conference. "I'm good. How did it go?"

"Productive, useful." He seems a little preoccupied. "Are you busy this evening?"

"No, free as a bird." I try to sound upbeat, but my voice doesn't ring true.

"I'm going to a talk. It's about sleep problems really, but it will also go into detail about the various stages of sleep. I think it might be of interest to you. I was given two tickets and I wondered if you'd like to come along?"

"That sounds great. What time?"

"I'll pick you up at six-thirty?"

What's actually going through my mind is Sheena's reference to BSBs and I feel uncomfortable. Then I get a grip. It's not a date. It's merely a lecture he thinks I'll enjoy.

"Thanks for thinking of me." At least my words reflect a genuine thank you.

"It's entirely my pleasure. See you in short while." The line goes dead and I find myself looking down at the phone. He's not an overly polite sort of guy, because he focuses on the practical side of life. He often forgets the commonplace niceties that other people think of as essentials. The fact that he's making an effort is worrying, but I realise that time is short if I'm going to have any chance of making myself look presentable. With messy hair and jogging bottoms and tee-shirt, I look like I've dragged myself out of bed. In fact I've been on the computer writing since six a.m. and Ethan was right, it's cathartic. Letting my emotions spill out onto the page is a harsh wake-up call, but after each session I feel calmer. There's almost a sense of relief and release. Once the words are there in black and white they aren't quite so insistent inside my head. I know I have to thank Ethan for his guidance.

Chapter Nine – Just Another Rainy Day

As I shower and dress I keep thinking about what Sheena said. She's right in one way, as I am lonely, and yet it isn't easy for me to open up to new people. The crowd I work with in my day job have no idea that I'm a medium and I need to keep it that way. It's less complicated and means that I'm not dragged into awkward conversations. There are three different points of view: those who believe, those who don't, and those in the middle. People who don't believe often feel they have to challenge you the moment it comes up in conversation. I refuse to be drawn into those sorts of discussions as it can become very heated. People start going on about proof, as if that means something. It makes me shake my head, although I should know better and that it's simply not their time to gain an understanding. It becomes annoying though, to say the least.

That leaves me with only my personal life to talk about. As my psychic work takes up the vast majority of my time outside of the office, there's little I can meaningfully discuss. I need to have some sort of life and the only way I'm ever going to do that is to socialise. I need to mix with normal people. The thought of having Ethan as a friend sort of defeats the purpose but, then again, it's probably safer. The more I think about it, the more I see that maybe I should let down my guard a little when I'm with him.

I push any thoughts of Alex away. I've learnt that I can't allow myself to let him seep back into my thoughts for even one moment, because he is my Achilles heel.

***

"Oh, you've dressed up," Ethan says as he steps through the door.

I instinctively put my hand up to my hair, wishing I hadn't bothered to scoop it up into a clip. Perhaps it looks a little too formal.

"I thought with the rain I'd play safe. I don't want to end up looking like I've been dragged through a bush backwards." I laugh to cover my self-consciousness. Ethan doesn't usually make personal comments

"Don't mind me, I was teasing." He steps inside, looking rather uncomfortable.

"Where are we heading?" I grab my bag and begin slipping on my coat. Ethan steps forward to hold it for me.

My heart misses a beat. If this is a date, I'm not sure I'm ready… despite mulling things over after Sheena's little talk.

"The other side of town. It's a twenty-minute drive to Charlton Hall, which is a great venue, and there will be drinks and canapés." He holds open the door for me and follows behind. As I lock the door he bends to pick up my bag which I dropped at my feet, and stands there holding it for me. When I take it from him with an awkward thanks, our hands touch and I freeze.

I look up at him: he's at least a foot taller than me and I wish I'd worn heels instead of flat shoes. As we walk to the car he makes polite conversation, and I wonder if he's regretting asking me along. It doesn't flow easily, but I think that's more to do with the fact that I feel so self-conscious.

"Look, Ceri," he says, stopping to turn around and gaze down at me. He frowns, furrowing his brow as if he's battling with a tough decision. "I hope I didn't put you on the spot about tonight. I genuinely think this will be an interesting talk, but there's another reason why I called you. I sometimes struggle to have normal friendships, with women. Heck, that makes me sound like I'm some crazy guy. What I mean is—"

I put up my hand to stop him. "I know exactly what you mean. It's the same for me. In fact, my best friend has been lecturing me about it today. Being serious all the time makes for a dull life, but in our line of work that isn't easy. We are both in the same position, Ethan, so let's not feel awkward. Everything happens for a reason, so let's enjoy an evening out. Drinks and canapés sound perfect to me, and I'm actually very interested in learning more about stages of sleep." I give him a rueful smile, and he laughs out aloud.

"I'm not much good at this, am I?" he jests.

It's enough to clear the air and we manage to chat away quite happily on the drive. He tells me a bit about his family and his ex. He has one son who is six and he really misses him, as he only manages to see him in the school holidays. His partner moved back to be with her family and it's a five hour journey each time he visits.

"I'm sorry it's so messy." I genuinely feel for him.

"How about you? Are you surviving?" He glances at me and then looks straight at the rear view mirror as he indicates and pulls into a car park.

"I manage one day at a time. Sheena thinks I've closeted myself away, and I have to say that loneliness is an awful thing. But sometimes it's easier than having to put all that effort into making new friends. Sorry, I wasn't referring to you, of course. I suppose it's different though, as we know quite a bit about each other already. It's easier filling in the gaps, if you follow my drift. You probably know more about the other side of me than even Sheena does. That does feel a bit strange, but it's actually a good thing."

He raises one eyebrow as if I've said something surprising. "Couldn't have put it better myself. We oddballs have to stick together."

The easy banter continues as we head inside. It's a large Georgian house set on probably an acre of land. It's now used entirely for corporate functions by the looks of it. The car park is huge and well laid out. We enter a grand reception area, and there are three different talks taking place. We drop our coats off at the cloakroom and wander through in search of The Clarence Suite.

I'm actually quite pleased that I took a little trouble with my appearance and opted for a little black dress. Ethan looks smart but casual in his jeans, pale blue shirt, and navy jacket. We check the meetings board and the talk is in one of the side rooms on the ground floor. The room can probably hold around eighty people. It has an enormous glass chandelier hanging elegantly from the ceiling, which is slightly off centre. It's clear this was originally one half of a much larger room. I think it would have been a magnificent ballroom once. On the other side of what is now a dividing wall is probably an exact mirror image of this room.

"Great place, isn't it?" Ethan stoops to whisper into my ear, but I notice he doesn't move in too close. He grabs two tulip-stemmed glasses off a silver tray and nods for me to move on into the room to find a seat. "Over there, on the right? Near the back, just in case it's boring and we can slope off early."

I shush him as a few heads turn and look in our direction, but I don't think anyone heard what he said. His voice is quite deep and he is an attractive looking man, I've noticed women often look his way. His height too, gives him an instant presence.

"Well." He settles into his seat and has to push his chair back to accommodate his legs. "Thanks for coming along, Ceri. I hope it's going to be worthwhile." He hands me a glass and we both take a sip, then immediately place our glasses under our chairs. Trying not to grimace, he shrugs his shoulders and heads off, returning with two glasses of orange juice instead.

The talk is fascinating. Professor Karl Shultz is impressive. I will admit that when we looked at the three events displayed on the board in reception: Sleep Disorders, Keeping Fit & Active over 60 and Marketing & Consumerism, I was tempted to turn around and keep walking. I immediately assumed that this was going to be a rather dry presentation with lots of pie charts, statistics and references to detailed research work. Well, it was all of those things in small measure, but this man is completely fascinating to listen to and watch. His body and hands never stop moving. He's passionate about the subject and his energy, and aura, is incredible. His vibration level in the ethereal world must surely be on a par with my own, although clearly he isn't an angel. He's simply an energy who has been working here on earth for a long time.

Stress is a direct result of the way life here works. It doesn't exist anywhere else, and the moment Karl Shultz steps out onto the small raised platform at the front of the room, I connect with him. He probably doesn't sense it: his ethereal side is reserved for deep sleep, and the irony of that isn't lost on me. His work is obviously to educate people and try to alleviate some of the unnecessary suffering. I glance at Ethan to gauge his reaction. Clearly he's impressed, although I'm not so sure he can see everything in quite the same way I can.

Whilst a great deal of the talk revolves around sleep disorders, his introduction gives detailed background on the various stages of sleep. I have to stifle a laugh, wondering if he will mention that it is only in deep sleep that we all return to the ethereal plane. I give Ethan a sideways glance at that point and he has to turn away from me, as a laugh is brewing. He comes back with a glare that says *behave yourself.*

I've never really understood the differences between the various stages of sleep. I suppose I look at it simplistically. You are either asleep or you are awake.

Professor Shultz explained that originally there were four non-REM stages, with REM being the fifth stage. However, over time two of the stages were combined. The science of how it works had never interested me before; but as he continued it explained many of the problems I'd experienced when working with people via their dreams. Much of the healing and guidance I do happens in the non-REM stages, as these can be remembered by the individual. What happens in the REM stage cannot, simply because this is one of the rules of the universe. Science seems to bear this out, without understanding the reasoning behind it.

What I'd often assumed was someone withdrawing from me, was in fact a part of the natural sleep process taking them further away from me and towards REM sleep. They weren't being unreceptive, but were simply affected by rhythmic brain activity, their heart rate slowing and their muscles relaxing as they moved through the sleep cycle. We exit the room after a wild round of well-deserved applause. I turn to Ethan and start saying how impressed I am and how glad I am that he invited me along, when the look on his face stops me mid-sentence. I turn to follow his gaze and am stunned to see Alex standing a few feet away. He looks shocked and very pale. The eye contact between the three of us is frantic. No one knows how to react. Ethan pulls himself together and turns me around, gently leading me outside.

My legs don't want to work and he ends up putting his arm around my waist to support me. I turn my head to look back at Alex, but one glimpse and he's gone. I lean into Ethan in despair.

Ethan leads me to a quiet bench and then heads back inside. He returns with two glasses of wine.

"Here," he places a glass firmly in my hand, "you need this. I'm sorry about that Ceri, I had no idea Alex would be here. It wasn't planned, this wasn't a trap. Alex is devastated, I can't believe this has happened. He assumed I'd taken you to a psychic talk and he told me he was working. He is, I just didn't know it was at the marketing talk here tonight."

I can feel he's mad with himself, but there's also something else: confusion. Everything happens for a reason, but why now, when the pain is beginning to lessen? Well, I say that lightly, as if it means something. It doesn't, but after all these months you learn to quietly accept what you can't change. Poor, poor Alex.

Ethan's mobile kicks into life and he checks the caller ID. He rolls his eyes. "Sorry, I have to answer this, it's Jess". He immediately stands and begins pacing back and forth. Clearly it's not good news. The call ends and he walks back towards me looking ashen.

"My son has been admitted to hospital with suspected appendicitis. They are taking him down to the operating theatre now." He stands there, not sure what to do.

"Go. Your son needs you. I can call a taxi. You have a long journey and you will want to be there when he wakes up."

Ethan looks relieved. He thanks me and leans forward to kiss my cheek. "I hate leaving you like this," he admits, and I can see he feels torn. Something else is unsettling him, but I give him a hug and say "Go. Be a daddy."

I sit for a while after Ethan's car disappears out of the car park. I can't face drinking the wine and walk back inside with it. I approach the reception desk to book a taxi and within a minute or two a small queue forms. Another of the talks has just finished. A woman standing directly behind me in the queue touches my arm, and leans forward. She asks whether I would mind sharing, she's overheard me giving my address and says she lives on the other side of the park.

"I don't like travelling on my own at night," she offers, apologetically. It's rather nice to have some company and I ask the driver to drop me off on the corner of the street, bidding my companion goodbye.

I walk slowly, deep in thought. As I approach the building I begin searching for my keys and when I turn my head to delve inside my bag, I glimpse a shadow. I snap back into the moment and begin walking a little faster. It's hard to tell, without turning around and staring, whether this is a real person or a spirit. The traffic on the main road obscures the sound of footfall, despite the lateness of the hour. It isn't fear I'm feeling though, no, it's something very different that I can't quite explain. I hurry inside the building and close the door firmly behind me, but as I step into the lift I hear the door click open. Whoever it is has the security code, so I relax a little, but the feeling in the pit of my stomach remains, like a ball of nervous energy.

The front door to the apartment opens on the first turn of the key and I step inside, feeling slightly breathless. For some unexplained reason I don't reach for the light switch. I drop my bag and jacket on the floor and stand for a moment in the twilight. The moonlight streaming in through the sitting room windows filters into the hallway. I realise the door didn't click behind me and I wonder why I was so careless, but my feet refuse to move. I could easily push it shut, simply by stretching out my hand, but something prevents me, even when I see a shadow hovering in the hallway. It steps inside. The door closes and I find myself standing within inches of the one man I can't resist.

We don't speak. Alex wraps his arms around me and pushes me gently back against the wall. His mouth is hot on my neck and I find myself holding my breath. My legs feel shaky and I'm glad to have the wall behind me for support. His body presses up tight against mine and there isn't one part of my body that isn't on fire.

As our lips find each other, I close my eyes and the voice is in my head. "Be careful, you are doing the work of an angel, but you have the temptations of a mortal." It's real enough for me to know I'm being guided, but every single cell in my body is screaming I want this, I need this man...

Alex scoops me up into his arms and carries me through to the bedroom. He lays me gently on the bed and stands over me. Even in the gloom I can see his face is full of love and passion. As I tug off my clothes, he drops his shirt on the floor and our eyes don't leave each other for a second. It seems like moments before we are lying next to each other and this isn't about right or wrong, fate or making mistakes. Rules mean nothing. This is about us and at this precise moment it's bigger than fate or the universe. Like a thief in the night, Alex has stolen my heart again, but this time he's taken my soul as well. Whatever the price I'm going to have to pay, it doesn't matter anymore.

We awake just before dawn. I'm not sure who stirs first, but suddenly our eyes are open and we're gazing at each other. Not one single word has passed our lips in the time we've been together. Words are inadequate, and what could we say to each other? We both sit up and I look at Alex nervously. He looks back at me with sad eyes, full of sorrow and pain. He leans forward, kisses my forehead and within minutes he's dressed and walking out the door.

I am incapable of moving, so full of distress at the emptiness he's left behind him. Not just from the loss of his physical presence, but the love and desire that filled this room which is now totally desolate. My body still tingles with the joy of loving the only man with whom I can be whole. The places he touched, the kisses and caresses, already memories of pleasure that might never be revisited. My mind relives the feel of his body, the warmth of his skin and the firmness of taught muscle as passion swept us both away. I let out a wail, like an animal in distress, and the sound is barely human. If the ethereal plane hasn't already registered my transgression, it will sense my pain now. My heart has been wrenched from my body yet again and I don't know how much more I can take. I shiver, as it dawns on me that I did nothing. I let him walk away... I let him walk out of my life as if he doesn't belong. Just a thief in the night.

Alex

Chapter Ten – Accepting The Inevitable

I feel feverish. Whether it's the adrenalin, or fear, I don't know. A dry sob wracks my body and the pain feels like there's a huge lump of iron stuck inside my chest.

Like a drug addict, I'm full of self-loathing because I fed my addiction, but it doesn't only hurt me: it hurts the woman I love. How could I be so selfish? I hear a key turn in the lock. Alicia is back and she'll wonder where I've been. I glance at the clock. It's just after eight in the morning, so she's probably been down to the local store to pick up milk or something for breakfast. I quickly grab the clothes I dropped so carelessly on the floor and head into the bathroom, locking the door behind me.

I switch on the shower, then turn and stand in front of the basin, staring into the mirror. As I pull off my clothes I take stock of what I see reflected before me. Man, you're in hell and you look like it. My body is mottled, almost bruised in places from the passionate clinches as Ceri clung to me. I've just spent an entire night making love to an angel. I disgust myself. I couldn't even speak to her, because if I did it would have been to say one thing:

"I don't care about what's right or wrong anymore."

***

I can't face work, even though I'm now freelance and all I have to do is take six strides and I'm at my desk. Pathetic. The day passes and sounds of the outside world filter in through the partially open window, serving only to remind me that everyone else is functioning normally.

By mid-afternoon I need to get up, my body is sore from lying in bed. I force myself to go out for a five-mile run, leaving the iPod behind because my head is already too full of stuff to tolerate music. I don't think, I try to switch off and let the rhythm of my feet pounding on the pavement calm me. When I begin to lapse, and thoughts creep back in, I run faster until the cramp is so painful I have to drop down onto a bench at the side of the road. It's chilly today and I cool down very quickly.

Suddenly, I hear my name. I spin around and there's someone standing back against the tall hedges behind the seat.

I blink and they are gone. Turning back around my mouth is still open. I was about to ask how they knew my name. As I sink back against the bench there's a pressure on my shoulders that feels slightly uncomfortable. Like someone has grabbed me, albeit with mild force, but as I grow accustomed to the feeling I find it strangely relaxing. A sensation of warmth spreads up my shoulders and into my neck, creeping up and over my head. I close my eyes.

How long I've been sitting here, I don't know, but my arms are covered in goose bumps as the sweat has chilled in the cool air. I feel like I've been asleep, but because I didn't wear my watch I have no idea of the time and decide to jog back home at a gentler pace.

As soon as I unlock the door, Alicia calls out to me.

"You're back." Her voice is full of concern. "Are you okay?" She walks out of the kitchen, drying her hands on a towel. "Coffee?"

"Please. I'll jump in the shower. Back in five minutes."

I shower and change. Walking back into the sitting room I feel relaxed and less stressed.

"I'm glad you're running again." She smiles at me, anxiously.

"I think I need to settle back into my old routine again. I become lazy when I don't exercise. Thanks." I take the coffee mug Alicia hands to me. She's looking brighter these days and it's good to see. "How was your evening?"

"Great! I'm meeting up with a couple of people from work tonight, down at the local pub. Do you fancy coming along?"

"No, you go and enjoy yourself. I'm going to work. I've taken too much time off lately and that has to change now. Life doesn't owe me anything and I've been acting as if it does."

She looks at me, shocked, and I realise it sounds a little harsh.

"I mean, I'm running behind on some deadlines and now I'm working for myself I have a reputation to build. I can't expect my clients to wait while I sort myself out."

I'm not sure the explanation helps, Alicia's face still registers concern, but she doesn't say any more.

I carry my coffee through to the study and it's three in the morning before I pull myself away from the computer to slink into bed, exhausted.

Chapter Eleven – Turning The Corner

What triggers a change in any person? Does it have to be something monumental, or can it be a few very small incidents that add up to a revelation? Seb, Ethan, and even Ceri, have been directing me to take control of my life and move on. Alicia still needs support but, even with the battles she has to face every single day of her life, she finds time to offer me advice or simple encouragement.

Now I'm back in my working and exercising groove, I feel I have a sense of normality. I don't give myself time to think, I do something instead. That means I'm flying through the work projects and clients are really beginning to sit up and notice me. No one ever submits something ahead of a deadline, but I'm on the case now and I work late into the night to ensure I deliver well before time.

There is a sense of satisfaction from picking up the pieces and trying to claw my way out of the mess that I made.

I begin putting things right by talking to Ethan. I rang him to find out how his son was doing, since that fateful night when I bumped into him and Ceri.

"Ethan, its Alex. How did the operation go?" I feel like a heel, knowing that's not the reason why I'm calling, although I really do hope his son is over the worst.

"Great, he's doing well, thanks for asking. They managed to

operate before it actually burst. Jess's parents have offered to put me up for the weekend, as Aaron is coming home late Friday afternoon. How are things with you? I can't apologise enough for what happened. I explained to Ceri it wasn't staged and she seemed to accept that. It only happened because I had been given two tickets and I knew Ceri would find the talk interesting. It wasn't a date, I know it looks bad now I come to think of it—"

"Ethan, it's none of my business. I'm moving on now and realise that's something I should have done months ago."

There's a moment's silence and the awkwardness is tangible. So he fancies Ceri.

"Look, I contacted her a while back after you and I chatted, I stuck to pretty much what you wanted me to ask her. After that it was work related. We move in the same circles and we couldn't avoid each other forever. You know my situation. I can't get involved with another woman because my ex, Jess, is very insecure at the moment and not happy to be back living with her parents. It's been hard for her, well, for both of us. Ceri is a great person, but she's not looking to hook up with anyone and neither am I at the moment."

He's given himself away. "At the moment" sounds like a warning shot to me. Okay, this really *is* none of my business, as I can't repeat the mistake I made the other night.

"I think Ceri might appreciate spending time with you, she must be lonely. I have to go, I'm on a tight deadline today. I'll catch you later and I'm glad Aaron is on the mend."

I wonder briefly if something in me has died. I feel disconnected from the emotion I know is there, after hearing Ethan talking about Ceri. He's getting to know her well in a work situation. Ha! Where have I heard that before? A man is supposed to be strong. Well, maybe I've learnt my lesson and my heart now has a shield around it. What better match for an angel, but a man who is a spiritual teacher? My fist makes a ball, but instead of pounding on my chest it comes to rest very gently over my heart. Ceri deserves happiness, no matter where it comes from, and there's no point in feeling bitter. Ethan is probably the person I would choose to be with her.

I'm done with overthinking things. Now I'm simply moving forward one step at a time.

Ceri

Chapter Twelve – Facing My Demons

I knew it was wrong. I move the mouse down over the list of folders and click on Spam. The number next to the heading reads two hundred and forty-eight in brackets. As I scan down I can only find a handful that aren't from Alex, until the day after our illicit night together. Something has changed and there is now one solitary email, which is already forty-eight hours old.

I hover over it. It was sent at 3.23 AM. My hand clicks before I have time to think about what I'm doing.

A cold chill runs down my back. I look at the words without reading them, as if they are merely hieroglyphics, patterns on the page. My eyes focus and the colour drains from my face.

We're done and I know it. It's over. A relationship can't be solely about the passion, it has to be a two-way street where both parties are fully committed. I don't know what came over me and I sure as hell don't know what came over you. Throwing me out at the start would have been a good move, unless you couldn't resist one last goodbye and it's my fault for making it impossible for you.

So this is me signing out. Ethan's a great guy. You are both on the same wavelength. I hope for your sake fate smiles on you

both, because he's had a rough time too. You both deserve better in this life, never mind about the next one.

Alex

I read it, then read it again and again. At first it stings more than a slap in the face, then I think it can be read in two very different ways. He's telling me to move on and he's blaming himself.

Tears obscure my vision and when I wipe my eyes I see that I've deleted the entire contents of the spam folder. I put my head down on the desk and sob. We're done and, this time, it really is for good.

***

Having successfully brought Alicia and Alex together I wasn't expecting a reward, but maybe some respite from the hell of human emotions might have been a nice gesture. Instead, the days following Alex's email are filled with a whole range of ugly thoughts and feelings. Bitterness doesn't even begin to describe it. I rant and rave, shout and scream, but nothing helps. No one comes to my rescue – whether that's ethereal or mortal. Does anyone care if I go mad inside these four walls? Where is Seb or Sheena? They are busy living their lives and five days pass with no contact from anyone. I sink into a depression.

Sunday morning there's a knock on the door. I drag myself up to answer it, putting the chain on so I can only open it a few inches. I look a mess and am in no fit state to take in someone's parcels.

"It's Ethan, Ceri. Let me in, I need to speak to you. Please."

I have to steel myself to unhook the chain, knowing full well he'll be shocked at what he sees. I open the door and walk back through into the sitting room. He closes the door quietly and follows me in. There's no loud exclamation, no pointed comments about the state of the room or the mess I'm in. Instead he puts both of his arms around me and holds me. Even when the tears have stopped, he continues to hold me. When the strength goes from my legs he lifts me up and lays me down on the sofa. Two minutes later he's back with a cold, wet flannel for my forehead, then he disappears again.

"Here. Hot, sweet tea, and don't say you don't want it, because you are going to do as I say. I'm only sorry I've been away spending time with Aaron. I should have realised there isn't anyone at hand to talk through what happened."

Ethan means bumping into Alex. My mind flashes back and I'm looking up into Alex's eyes as he lowers his body onto mine. Ethan shakes me.

"Ceri, drink this tea. Now. It's an order." He physically picks up my legs and swings me around into a sitting position.

"How did you know I wasn't well?"

"You didn't turn up for the event last night, but don't worry, I covered for you. I went along because I wanted to surprise you. It turned out you surprised me."

His voice is hard. He doesn't suffer fools gladly and I'm a fool. Ethan has a deep well of sympathy, but he won't waste it on people who won't help themselves.

"Ceri." He looks at me sharply. "Do you think you are the only person to suffer? You of all people should abhor the waste of self-pity. Depression is a luxury you can't afford. You should be helping other people who aren't as well equipped to cope as you are."

I reel from his words. He's right, and guilt wraps its ugliness around me.

"I need a shower." I swallow the rest of my tea and pass him the cup. "I'll be back shortly."

He watches me as I walk away, then I hear him opening the door into the kitchen. I return fifteen minutes later, refreshed, dressed, and with my hair neatly brushed and pulled back in a ponytail. The smell of bacon wafts past my nose.

"There isn't much in the fridge. I'm defrosting some bread for some bacon sandwiches. I need to talk to you about a few work-shops I'm arranging. I want you to take part."

He acts as if nothing has happened. I'm not sure what I was expecting, but I think this is precisely what I need. My only concern is, why is Ethan the only one who understands?

Alex

Chapter Thirteen – Escaping Into My Dreams

Life is easy. I work hard and the business is growing. Success brings money, which doesn't concern me, but it's also making me see that not everything I touch falls apart. I can be successful in something. I don't wake in the morning feeling depressed anymore, although there's a good reason for that.

I spend my nights with Ceri.

I can't remember one night since that final time together when she hasn't filled my dreams. I can touch her skin, breathe in the scent of her body, and I'm there with her. It's enough to keep me going, because I know that before the day is out we will be together again.

Alicia more or less has her own life now and I'm pretty sure she will be moving out soon. I've felt privileged to be here for her during her split with Niall, when she faced up to the fact that she doesn't need a man in her life. She's a competent woman and I truly believe the hurt within her is healing. She went to see Ethan for a private sitting and afterwards she wouldn't tell me what happened. It was clear when I picked her up to bring her home that she had been crying. Her cheeks were dry, but her eyes were puffy and red. Whatever messages he gave her, she was different after that. I gave her the opportunity to talk about it, but all she would say was that nothing is lost forever and understanding that had helped.

While it's been nice to have company and to feel I've helped a little, I won't be too sorry to lose my flatmate. I know she's moving on to begin again and appreciates the fact that I gave her the space she needed at a crucial point in her life.

Seb contacts me frequently, but we don't talk about Ceri anymore. He's enjoying his new job and now goes out in the field as well as being part office-based. I think it's important to him that he doesn't lose touch with the harsh reality of the job. His input means things really do happen out there on the ground and people's lives are changed in a very real way. He mentioned he's involved in some fundraising over here and I offered to help out if he thought there was anything I could do.

Sheena emails me from time to time. It's always light and friendly. Neither of us ever mentions Ceri.

However, there's one last thing I have to do. I've been putting it off for quite a while. Ethan and I lost touch: it was too painful talking to him knowing that he's the man in Ceri's life now. Eventually I let go of my jealousy because it was eating me alive, and that was liberating. I can now think of Ceri and smile, instead of wanting to hammer down her door like a caveman and claim my woman. Basic instincts are hard to ignore, but there's a real sense of triumph in proving that you are in control. I can do this for her. If I could just see her, to know that he's made her happy, then I could be at peace.

I look at my watch and smile. Another fourteen hours and we'll be together in my dreams. No one can take that away from me, not even fate.

***

My head hits the pillow and the sheets feel cool against my skin.

The darkness is comforting. I imagine the stress of the day flowing down through my body and out through my feet, willing my muscles to relax. My mind calls out to her.

Ceri, Ceri, come be with me. I'm here and I'm waiting for you.

I start to breathe deeply, holding each breath and expelling it slowly, counting in a rhythm that lulls my mind.

It's a bright morning, very early, and I turn when I hear her footsteps. She smiles at me shyly and wraps her arms around me. It's gentle and I kiss her shoulder, then lift her hand so that my lips can work down her arm. I kiss her finger tips and hold her hand to my cheek.

"I missed you." My voice is hoarse with emotion.

"I'm always here. I never leave you. If you relax you will feel me. Our hearts are entwined because we are one." She smiles up at me from beneath brown lashes. The breeze lifts her hair and she absentmindedly brushes it away from her eyes.

"I believe you, but it's hard at times. I feel I don't belong here anymore. No one understands me, only you, my love."

Her eyes are sad and she holds me tight against her. "Come, walk with me. Let go of your negative thoughts. Here we can always be true to ourselves, and that's my gift to you. Never fear, you do not walk alone."

Our hands lock. The warmth of her flesh reassures me and, as we walk, I wonder if this is heaven.

Chapter Fourteen – Happiness Is Seeing The Person You Love Smiling

I had my final glimpse of Ceri. They say everything happens for a reason, well, this one was too big a coincidence not to have a much deeper meaning. I think the universe decided to throw me a break. Did I deserve it? Well, I think the jury is still out on that one. You see, I sent her an email. Well, it was probably the three hundredth one, or something, but it was special. I doubt she opened any of the others, but after our final, totally unplanned night together I knew she would give in. Did I declare my undying love? Tell her how much being with her excited me and made me feel fulfilled? No, I alienated her in the only way I could think of that would allow her to let us go. It was the point of no return, so I wasn't surprised when I was granted this one last thing.

I don't mix in psychic circles, so I have no idea when either Ethan or Ceri are in town for the regular clairvoyant events. To be honest I'm terrified by it all now, and I don't know what I believe anymore. So it's the last place I would go, even to satisfy myself that Ceri's life is a happy one.

I was skimming the local paper over a leisurely Saturday morning breakfast and I saw it, an advert for a fun run in aid of charity. There was a photo of Ethan and Seb, then some photos of the overseas projects Seb has been involved with. Ceri was mentioned by name in the article and it seems they have also been raising funds by selling tickets to special psychic events. I won't pretend a part of me didn't feel gutted that I wasn't the one chosen to help Seb and Ceri, but Ethan is a good man.

I've come to terms with the fact there was absolutely nothing I could have done differently, that it wasn't my fault and I didn't fail. It was never meant to be, but for a while the bitterness and longing ruled my head and my actions. I've had no choice but to become a stronger person and that final email was my gift to Ceri. The depth of her love meant she would never let go, and our final night confirmed that. She didn't hold back for one second, she abandoned everything she believed in without fear or thought. It was enough for me and I will always treasure that knowledge.

In my attempt to move on I've had a few dates with one of my clients. It started with a meeting over a drink and progressed to a few meals out when we're both free. It's very casual at the moment, as she has a four year old daughter and she's understandably cautious. Macy knows I'm still very raw from the breakup of my previous relationship, but she doesn't know any of the details. It suits us both at the moment and it's a way of socialising without feeling any undue pressure.

I asked her if she was interested in taking part in a fun run and she loved the idea. Macy offered to complete our application and did it in her name with a plus one. As I said, it was too big a coincidence to be merely that.

It was a huge turnout with over two thousand people congregating at the starting line in the park. It was easy to be invisible in the throng of runners clustered in groups as everyone warmed up. Macy is easy to chat to and for the first time in quite a while I felt like a normal guy having fun doing something he enjoys. I kept scanning the sea of faces, not lingering on any one in particular in case I found myself eye to eye with Ceri.

It wasn't until after the race began that I saw Ceri and Ethan.

We set off in small groups and as people slowed their pace on the uphill hauls, the groups dispersed and spread out. I sensed her presence before I saw her, something inside me kicking my senses. They were pacing themselves, running side by side, and every now and again they glanced at each other and smiled. I could tell that Ethan was watching her like a hawk, making sure she was running at a comfortable pace. Macy and I began gaining ground, so I had to fake a cramp in my calf muscle to avoid getting too close to them. We stopped at one of the drinks stations and Macy good-naturedly marked time running on the spot while I grabbed some water and did a few stretches. Then we were off again, but I made sure our pace meant we were far enough behind Ceri and Ethan not to be noticed by either of them.

"I've enjoyed today," Macy said when we said goodbye. "You're the first guy I've dated who shares a love of running. My ex was into the gym and was obsessed with lifting weights, but he wouldn't do anything that involved being out in the fresh air." She frowned.

"Oh, the heavy stuff! I admire the dedication, but for me it would be too boring. I enjoy nature and I love being out in the fresh air, so what's not to like?"

She studied my face as if seeing something new in me that interested her. "My thoughts exactly." She smiled. "We must do this again. Maybe not such a long distance next time."

We parted company with our usual smile and a wave, but she hesitated and I wondered if she wanted me to hug her. I'm not ready, yet. Maybe one day soon, but not today. In the car driving home I kept picturing Ceri's face. She looked tanned and happy. When she smiled at Ethan her eyes lit up, as they had when I first knew her and before things became so mixed up. I replayed her smile over and over in my head, like the frames from a series of camera shots... it's just a pity the person she was smiling at was another man.

Enough, Alex! She's happy and that's all you needed to know. I said a silent thank you to whoever had taken pity on me. Then I turned my attention to the next project I was about to start working on later this afternoon. Finally I'm in a place where everything feels neutral, no excessive highs or lows, and that's a good point to build a new future from.

***

The following morning I awake with a start from a deep sleep. I open my eyes and the daylight is harsh, making me squint. I turn onto my side to replay my dream, except that there's nothing there, no memory of being with Ceri to start my day. It's the strangest feeling and I'm truly lost, set adrift in a world I no longer understand. I drag myself out of bed and into the shower to stop the sensation of panic rising in my chest.

Ceri

Chapter Fifteen – The Circle Of Life

Why did I think Ethan wasn't a patient man? He has been by my side constantly, either in person or on the phone, talking me through each day. Every single hurdle and setback I've had, he's listened and kept me moving forward. Without him I would have no focus. At times he's been hard on me, pushing me relentlessly and refusing to let me dwell on regrets and fears. We've grown closer in so many ways and a part of that is due to the fact he has shared all of his own fears with me. His son Aaron is the one thing in his life that brings him pure joy. He admitted that he always felt he'd failed his ex-wife, Jess, who hated the work he did. Towards the end they fought about it constantly. From what I've seen so far though, he drops everything whenever she needs something. Maybe they both need to accept the inevitable and move on.

A bitter laugh escapes my lips. Who am I to talk?

His work is fulfilling, but also full of frustrations. At least in that respect we can meaningfully share our trials and tribulations. Many of the people I help grab onto what is offered, but there are others who brush all help away. Human nature seems to encourage people to hold onto hurt and it is only having a belief that can break the endless circle. Ethan feels each disappointment acutely: he takes each rejection as a personal failure. He laughs at me, good-naturedly, as if I'm well-meaning but missing the point.

"We're on different levels, Ceri. There's so much I don't understand, so I can't look at things in quite the same way that you do," he admits in a regretful tone. There's so much I can't tell him... it seems unfair.

I give up my part-time job and, if I'm honest, it isn't without a hint of sadness. However, there is no point in pretending that my future isn't going to be totally caught up in spiritual work. Ethan has pulled me into several projects which are rather exciting. Not least are a series of workshops and a fun run raising funds for the project Seb's involved with. I didn't realise how I'd pushed everyone away for a short while and it felt good to put that to one side and pick up the threads again.

Seb is going from strength to strength. He's happy and has a wide group of new friends. He never mentions anyone in particular, but I feel he has someone with whom he can talk meaningfully. I see that as a start and I know there is happiness for him in the future, although he will be on his own for a few years.

The doorbell rings and I take one last look in the mirror to check no stray tendrils of hair have escaped the hairclip and I smile back at the reflection I see. These days I am feeling more and more comfortable with the person I am in this life.

"Sheena, you're late."

She steps inside and we hug, her face is glowing.

"I have news...*big* news. I can't wait to tell you," she shrieks. I usher her inside and she literally throws her bag and coat down on the chair impatiently.

"Well?" I ask, my senses instantly picking up the vibe.

"I'm pregnant!" Her face is a picture of happiness and we hug like the sisters we have become.

"Oh my goodness! Congratulations, I can't believe it!"

She looks at me and chuckles. "You knew, didn't you?" she peers at me accusingly.

"Well, maybe I had an inkling. Coffee or juice?"

"Ah, juice please, I'm thinking healthily now. Can you really believe I'm going to be a mum?"

"And I'm going to be an aunt. It's about time someone had a baby, I can't remember the last time I held a newborn in my arms." As the words escape my mouth a tinge of regret courses through me, but I put it to one side. This is a time to be joyful and count our blessings, and a baby is a blessing indeed.

"How's Ethan?"

I hand Sheena her juice and stir my coffee. "Great. He's been amazing. The fundraising is going really well and we've had a lot of fun with the workshops. Each one has been sold out and the demand has been so great that once it's all over Ethan and I are going to run a regular series of sessions. It seems there are a lot of very stressed people out there looking for guidance on how to make significant changes in their lives. Not all of them are interested in mediumship and clairvoyance, so this is the perfect vehicle for them."

"I can understand people being cautious about the heavy spiritual stuff. I am too, so it's good to hear that the two of you are recognising that. Maybe I'll come along to one of your motivational meditation sessions. Is it a bit like Alcoholics Anonymous? Hello, my name is Sheena and I'm a compulsive workaholic, show me how to relax."

I start laughing and she joins in.

"I like to think it's a bit subtler, but in essence, you aren't far wrong. It's as if people are looking for someone to say it's okay to step back and not feel you have to be productive every second of the day. We've had some fantastic results already."

Sheena rests her elbows on the table and places her hands beneath her chin. She's in serious mode. "Have you slept with him yet?"

"Sheena! I can't believe you've asked me that. We're just good friends." My face colours, despite the fact that I'm trying to remain cool about our relationship.

"Oh, so you're thinking about it then," she dismisses my

comment and raises her juice glass to me in an air toast. "To the future," she says, with a wry smile on her face.

***

Sheena insisted that the four of us go out for a meal tonight and a quick call to Ethan confirms he's free. When he arrives there's something different about him. I think he's had his hair cut, or maybe it's because he's looking quite smart this evening. For one moment I have a flashback of Alex, which I dismiss as quickly as it comes. Ethan leans forward to kiss my cheek as I hold the door open for him.

"You look very smart," I can't help commenting.

"I thought I'd make an effort to impress your friends," he jokes, but I can see he's pleased I've noticed.

"Maybe I'll rethink what I'm wearing. I'll be back in a moment."

"I'll make coffee," he calls over his shoulder as he walks off towards the kitchen

I look at myself in the mirror and think how lacklustre I look. I slip off my jeans and top, then grab a couple of dresses from the cupboard. I hold each one up and then discard them. I remember something I bought a while ago that I've never worn. It's a plain knit dress, knee length in a deep purple, and I remember it felt good when I tried it on. As I delve into the back of the cupboard there's a knock on the door and I automatically say "come in". I spin around and realise I'm in my underwear, and I quickly grab the first thing to hand to cover myself.

Ethan stands there looking rather shocked, coffee mug in hand. His eyes sweep over me, slightly embarrassed, and then he turns away to put the hot drink down on a side table.

"Sorry," he mutters and exits as quickly as he can.

My heart is thumping and I feel both hot and cold at the same time. Don't be stupid, Ceri, I reprimand myself. It's unlikely you are going to go through life without another man looking at your body.

84

I find the purple dress and quickly pull it over my head. I run my hands down over my hair so that it's perfect again and grab the mug. Ethan is standing by the window, watching the traffic go by. He looks up the moment he hears the bedroom door open.

"Sorry," he apologises, unable to look me in the face.

"My fault, I forgot what I was doing and I told you to come in. It's no big deal."

His eyes meet mine and I give him an encouraging smile.

"That looks really good on you. Purple is your colour." He smiles back. It's a grateful smile, but then he frowns. "Ceri?"

"Yes?"

"Can I kiss you? I don't mean a peck on the cheek."

I don't know how I feel about this, but I guess I'll never know if I make an excuse. I walk towards him without answering his question. I put my mug on the table and then turn to face him. Standing on tip-toe I kiss him, and it's a real kiss. It lasts for several seconds and he kisses me back gently. He puts his arms around me to take the weight off my toes and as we pull apart he lowers me to the floor.

"Reaction?" He gazes down at me, his question honest.

"Nice," is the only word that springs to mind, and then I realise that might be a disappointment to him.

"Well, that's a start. I'll try harder next time."

He's sending me a message in very clear terms. There are two options and he wants me to consider how I feel about him before he makes his next move. I'm a little flustered because I'm not ready and I know I've purposely been avoiding thinking about it. I don't know how I feel about taking our relationship to the next level.

***

The pub is packed, but Sheena and Sam are already seated in a booth. It's the first time Sam and Ethan have met, and they shake hands before we all sit down. Sheena has an orange juice in front of her and there's an open bottle of white wine in a chiller with three glasses.

"Wine okay?" Sam asks, pouring out a glass. "Or would you prefer beer, Ethan?"

"Wine's fine," he confirms and I nod. "I hear congratulations are in order for your two, or should I say, three." Ethan holds up his wine glass and we toast. Sam and Sheena are all smiles and the buzz between them is awesome. Sheena is right, Sam was worth the wait. Ethan looks at me and raises his eyebrows, then touches his glass against mine.

"To good news and good times," he says. He places his glass on the table and then slips his hand over mine, which is resting on my leg. Sheena notices and her left eyebrow raises a fraction as she shoots me a glance.

"Pregnancy is an amazing journey, enjoy every moment. After they are born the years go by way too fast," Ethan says.

"You have children, Ethan?" Sam sounds surprised.

"One son, Aaron, with my ex, Jess. He's the best thing that ever happened to me, until I met Ceri."

Sam and Sheena raise their glasses to him in acknowledgement and I give a nervous laugh. Ethan squeezes my hand gently and then moves his arm gently around my shoulders. He's relaxed and happy. I tune out of the conversation around the table as two inner voices discuss the pros and cons of making my decision.

I feel like I'm watching everything through a window, like an interloper. Sheena and Sam are very much in love and in tune, happiness radiates from them both. A sideways glance at Ethan and I feel I'm seeing him for the first time. An attractive guy, he's amazingly gentle despite his tall and powerful frame. He has soft, curly black hair that never really looks groomed. He talks in an animated way, using his free hand to express himself, but content to have one arm curled protectively around me. He's happy to share Sheena and Sam's excitement and it's clear he's connecting with them in a very personal way. I don't think I've ever seen him this relaxed, or this carefree. One of my inner voices says decision time, Ceri, and I wonder if it's my subconscious voice, or whether I'm being guided. I lean in closer to Ethan and he instantly squeezes my shoulder, beaming down at me.

I think I've made my decision.

Chapter Sixteen – The Next Step

We all end up back at Ethan's place. Sam is a little tipsy from a few glasses of wine at the bar as Sheena is driving. Ethan and I only had a glass, the tension between the two of us mounting throughout the evening.

Ethan takes us through to the kitchen, which is on the ground floor of his three-storey house. Sheena hasn't been here before and enthuses over the décor, so Ethan suggests she and Sam do a tour. "There's a balcony on the top floor," he calls out to them, as they disappear into the hallway.

Ethan pushes the door so it's ajar, then turns to me. He places a hand on each shoulder and stares down at me intently.

"Have you made your decision? I don't think I can't wait any longer."

I take a moment, before raising my gaze to meet his.

"Do you feel this is the right move for us? I'm scared that I'll make another mistake and misread the signs. Maybe I'm supposed to be alone forever. I don't want to hurt you Ethan, not like—"

He places a finger against my lips to silence me, then lowers his head until his mouth is on mine. There's a powerful urgency to his kiss.

"I can't see your future, or mine, Ceri. You know how it works, but I'm not taking this lightly. We have to both feel the same, so no one gets hurt."

"Then I've made my decision."

"So you'll stay the night?"

I nod as the door swings open and Sam stumbles in.

"Nice place, Ethan," his words are slightly slurred, and Ethan immediately flicks the switch on the kettle and opens a cupboard to grab some mugs.

"Do you see yourself having more children, Ethan?" Sheena asks, as I take over making the coffee.

"At some point I would love to settle down and I think Aaron would love to have a sibling. At the moment he's surrounded by adults. His grandparents look after him when Jess is at work. He has a wide circle of friends, though." He flashes me a look.

"How about you, Ceri?" Sam asks.

It's an innocent enough question, and Sam doesn't know the circumstances. Sheena frowns and her demeanour says a silent "sorry, should have warned him".

"You never know what the future might hold. I think most people like to think they will be able to enjoy family life at some point. I'm not close with my own family, which my brother and I always thought was a shame. Families should be close."

It's an honest reply, although I don't think I've answered it the way Ethan might have hoped. He knows why I can't simply enthuse and say I'm looking forward to having children of my own. I can't control my destiny, it isn't up to me.

Sheena tactfully changes the subject and encourages Sam to drink his coffee quickly.

As we see them out she turns to hug me and holds it a second or two longer than normal. When she pulls away her eyes are tearful, but she says nothing.

Closing the door behind them, the house suddenly seems very quiet. Ethan grabs my hand and leads me upstairs.

"Sheena and Sam are a great couple. They're very lucky."

"They deserve each other and I'm thrilled for them both." My words come out a little breathless. I'm nervous.

"I meant what I said, Ceri, when I answered Sam's question. I'm ready to commit."

He pushes open his bedroom door. It's the first time I've been inside this room. It's very neutral, distinctly lacking in feminine touches, but everything is extremely neat and clean. There's a Zen theme going on and it's a tranquil setting.

I'm going through the motions, following Ethan's lead. He stops in front of the bed and turns to me, tipping back my chin with his hand so that he can stare into my eyes.

"Are you sure about this?"

"Yes, I'm sure."

He pulls down the zipper on the back of my dress and it falls to the floor. I step out of my shoes and lie back on the bed. He strips down to his boxer shorts and lowers himself down next to me. He rolls on his side and places a hand on my stomach, it feels strange. As he leans in to kiss me, he suddenly recoils sharply. A haunted look appears in his eyes.

"What?" I ask, dreading what he's going to say.

"This is all wrong, Ceri. I left it too late. What an utter fool I've been!" He rolls away from me to stand up and begins dressing.

"Ethan I don't understand...?"

"I'm still in love with Jess. I hope you can forgive me, Ceri, but I can't do this. I was scared because I thought you were the one who was going to back out. Talk about a revelation... I sure as hell didn't see this coming!"

Chapter Seventeen – Pride Comes Before A Fall

It wasn't until Ethan dropped me home that the relief flooded over me. Who was I trying to kid? Someone on the other side was protecting me from myself tonight. Maybe they were protecting Ethan's feelings as well. How could I try to fool myself like that, when I know what's still in my heart?

I stand under the shower, letting the water cleanse me as if it is washing away the vestiges of another big mistake. When I lie down on the bed I want to hasten into my dream state, there is a question I need to ask.

***

Transition now takes mere moments, living as I do with the ability to be on both sides of this earthly life with ease. I open my mind and know that my ethereal mentor is here for me.

"Why?"

"Because you were about to make big a mistake. You were using your head and not your heart, which was not only disappointing but totally out of character. You were taking the easy way out, Ceri."

"Can you blame me, given what I've been through?"

"Spoken like a true mortal. You are an angel. You are above the pulls of human emotions. You know better." His words sting.

"I've failed."

"Yes."

"How will I learn the new lessons so that I can move on and prove my worth?"

"You have succeeded in many of the tasks you have been set and we are pleased. You have already helped many people and will continue to do so. However, you have also presented us with an unexpected dilemma."

His words strike fear into my heart. I've tried to limit the damage I've done, but obviously it wasn't enough.

"I know I've done wrong. I wish I could say I would do it differently if I was given a second chance, but I cannot lie to you. Nothing prepared me for the feelings I have for Alex. I'm ashamed, but all I can say in my defence is that some emotions are so powerful they take over your mind, heart, and soul. My beliefs are still strong, but I was even stronger when I was with him."

"It's all academic now." The words are communicated without emotion.

"What do you mean?"

"You succeeded in changing your fate. What happens next is entirely up to you."

"But what about Alex?"

"His fate, too, lies in your hands. I'm here if you need me."

The silence inside my head is deafening.

***

It was the longest night of my life. I awoke and began pacing the floor. What does this all mean? Is my life now a blank page with regard to Alex? How can I steamroller into his life again after the pain I've caused him?

I sit at the kitchen table, my hands wrapped around a strong cup of coffee, in the early morning gloom. Little thrills of excitement keep coursing through my body and I have to try really hard to remain calm. What is the next step for me now? It's a little after four in the morning and I wander into the study.

I open up the laptop and go straight to the spam folder. It's full of junk and nothing from Alex. I click compose and type "I'm sorry" into the subject line. What should I say? For a long while I sit looking at the blank space in the body of the email. It glares back at me, as if to say there are no words to right this wrong. Is that true? Maybe this is about learning more than one lesson. If fate doesn't lay out the path in front of us, it suddenly becomes rather frightening to take a step into the unknown. My fingers begin typing and I'm eager to see what appears on the screen.

My darling Alex, I'm sorry. I love you,

I love you, I love you... can you forgive me? I will love you forever. C xxx

I have to lift my fingers away from the keyboard so that they will stop typing and add the word "forever". I press send without a moment's hesitation, knowing full well that it's probably too late. That might be the next lesson I'm being taught... be careful what you wish for, it might just come true. I can only hope my spirit guides continue to look out for me as I fight for Alex's love.

***

I have no choice but to pack my bag and head off to a psychic convention. I'm making a personal appearance and it's a three hour journey by train. It's in totally the opposite direction to where I want to be heading. It's taking me further away from Alex. I keep checking my emails, frantic when I lose the internet connection on my phone. Nothing. Maybe he isn't online today, or is he simply avoiding me? Is he sitting in front of the pc, my email in front of him and the cursor hovering over it, unable to decide whether to press open or delete?

The day passes, the evening passes, and after hours of agonizing I'm back in the hotel room. Still there's nothing from Alex. I pack my bag ready to leave early in the morning. I know he works from home most of the time and that's my next step.

***

There's no reply when I knock on the door. I ring the bell once, twice, three times, and eventually a neighbour comes out onto the landing.

"No one's home. He's been away for a couple of days." The woman eyes me suspiciously. I suppose I was hammering on the door and then pressing the doorbell frantically. It must look very suspicious.

"Oh, thank you. Do you know where Alex went?"

Clearly she has no intention of sharing anything at all with me. She looks me up and down as if she just caught me trying to break in.

"No. I don't know." She shuts the door and I'm left standing, not sure what to do next.

***

Another day passes. No emails and no reply when I call at Alex's apartment. I don't have his mobile number on my new phone, so I ring Sheena and ask if she can text it to me.

"Ceri, why on earth do you want Alex's number after all this time? It's kinder to leave the poor guy alone. I think he's seeing someone now," she says, gently.

"Alicia? No, it's not what you think. Ethan told me, she was just a flat mate. Alex wasn't sleeping with her, only helping out an old friend." I don't like hearing the desperation in my voice.

"This is a new friend. They were together at the fun run the other week. I didn't say hello or anything, but I saw them and they are clearly an item."

It's like the floor has opened up beneath my feet. It's too late and that is the lesson I'm being taught! I was warned a long time ago… don't change anything as the ripples spread out and the only one to blame here is me.

"You're sure about that? There's no mistake about them having a relationship?"

"Her name is Macy and she has a daughter. That's all I know."

I feel guilty for grilling Sheena, as I know she's only doing this out of sisterly love. "Just because they've been out together doesn't mean there's any commitment between them. This is too important for me to take anything at face value, Sheena."

"He told me himself, I'll send you the email. I thought you'd moved on... what about Ethan?"

"There never was anything other than friendship and shared interests between us. I know how it looked when we went out for dinner, but so much has happened since then. I can't explain now, I can't rest until I'm satisfied I've done everything I can. I will have to live with this for the rest of my life – whichever way it goes."

"The email is on the way. Good luck honey."

I disconnect and pick up the text, saving Alex's number to my contact list. After six rings it goes straight to voicemail.

What can I say? I press the end call button, knowing words are going to be inadequate. When I sit down in front of the laptop I have eighteen emails. None are from Alex, but one is from Sheena. I open it with trepidation.

From: Alex385ID71@pcit.com

To: cheerfulchic01@gmail.com

Re: Thanks for your support

Hey lady! Nice to hear from you and sorry I didn't spot you in the crowd of runners. I was with Macy. She's a client and fast becoming my significant other. We really enjoyed our day and the run was exhilarating. You couldn't have picked a better day for it. Unfortunately we can't make the next one, as it's Macy's daughter's birthday and I'll be meeting her for the first time.

Hope things are good with you.

Alex

I scroll down to read Sheena's original email to Alex.

From: cheerfulchic01@gmail.com

To: Alex385ID71@pcit.com

Thanks for your support

Hi Alex, I just wanted to thank you for coming along and supporting the cause. I caught a glimpse of you, but before I could make my way through the crowd, you were off and running again. I hope you can join the next fun run and maybe we can catch up.

Take care,

Sheena

My chin sinks down onto my chest and I gently expel the air from my lungs in one long, agonizing gasp. Alex's dream is about to come true. A woman who can love him without reservation or complication and a daughter to help fill the void he's always felt from the loss of his own biological child. I delete the email, then delete his number from my phone. Within seconds all hope has died, as I know I can't destroy his chance of happiness with someone who is at least normal. The fact that it isn't Alicia is probably my fault too. What other effects have rippled outwards because of my inability to accept my fate? I can't retract the email I sent, I can only hope it goes into spam and will be autodeleted along with all the other trash.

Chapter Eighteen – New Friendships And Strong Bonds

The one very positive aspect about the bad things in life is that the more knocks you receive, the easier it is to drag yourself back up from the floor the next time around. Alex doesn't respond to my email and I'm relieved. Why make a nightmarish situation any worse?

However, I have to see for myself that he's happy. I can't totally let go with good grace until I know for sure he's in a happy relationship, especially after the misunderstanding over Alicia moving in with him.

My plan is to hang around close to his apartment and follow him. Only until I can see for myself that he's really picking up his life in a meaningful way. I don't intend to interfere or complicate things, but I have to be one hundred per cent sure this time around.

Two days following, I'm there from seven in the morning, but there's no sign of him. As each day drags on I begin to wonder if he even lives there anymore.

Then, on day three a taxi pulls up at the kerb. A tanned, fit guy steps out and before he even has a chance to turn around, I know its Alex. He leans in to pay the driver and as the taxi pulls away he's left standing with two large suitcases and some hand luggage.

He's wearing a white straw panama hat and he looks so good I groan out aloud. Then I have to throw myself across the passenger seat, as his head turns in my direction. After a few minutes I look up, but he's already carrying the luggage inside.

I feel like a private investigator. Okay, he's been on holiday, but he could have gone on his own. He looks good… so good, that a tingly heat sensation begins in the pit of my stomach. Concentrate, Ceri. What do I do now? I sit and wait, watching for any sign of movement at the windows on the second floor. I spot him once or twice as he passes the bedroom window, no doubt unpacking his suitcase.

An hour and a half later and I'm thinking this is stupid. It's stalking. I'm just about to put the key in the ignition and go home to drown my sorrows with a bottle of wine, when he steps out into the street. He saunters down to the corner and heads in the direction of the local shops. I quickly follow him on foot, trying not to run to catch up, because I know he won't be going very far. I can take my time. I don't want to look suspicious, or draw his attention.

He's not in a hurry, but he has long legs and I have to take probably two steps to each one of his strides. It makes me feel very self-conscious and I draw a strange look from a young woman walking towards me. He stops a few times, once to take his wallet out of his pocket and he checks to see whether he has some cash. I have to jump behind a tree. If he turns his head slightly he will see me, despite the discreet distance I've been keeping. Where is everyone when you want to disappear into a crowd?

He isn't in the shop for very long and when he comes back out he has a small bag. It looks like milk, bread, and the usual things you need after you've been away from home. But he has one other, unexpected, item: a small white dog on a lead. As Alex walks off, talking to the dog, I recognise Geoff, the owner of the shop as he steps out and shouts after him. He walks briskly up to him and hands him a small bag, which I assume contains doggy things, and they both laugh. Alex juggles the two bags and the leash, shouting a "thanks" over his shoulder.

The dog begins pulling on the leash and Alex walks faster, but after a few moments the dog is really straining to push forward. Even from forty paces away I hear Alex's voice carry on the wind. "Harry, slow down. We're going home, boy."

The walk back is tortuous. How I wish I could sidle up to Alex and pass the time of day. To be able to engage him in conversation as if we were old friends bumping into each other. Instead I have to keep hiding behind things as the dog continues his stop/start journey homewards. He's a cute little dog, I think he's a Westie. He's pure white and has a very male gait to his walk, despite his little legs.

At the front door Alex has to juggle the shopping and the dog. It's all I can do to stop myself leaping out from behind the rubbish bins to open the door for him. Once he's inside that's it for him for the rest of the day. At eight o'clock I head for home, weary in mind and body.

***

I assume the next morning Alex will have a lie in, then take Harry for his morning walk. I arrive around seven-thirty and I'm right. Moments after I pull up he comes jogging around the corner, Harry trotting alongside him. His tee-shirt is sticking to him and his hair is flat to his head, but I can't take my eyes off him. He disappears inside and I see him pass the window maybe five or six times. It's a work day for Alex and I suspect he will be in the study most of the time. A few people come and go during the morning, but it's hard to tell if any of them are visitors. They are all male, so even if they are visiting him it's better than a succession of attractive women calling at the building. This isn't going to work. I could sit here for days and still not know what's happening in his life.

It's too obvious to involve Seb or Sheena. I can't approach Ethan as I don't think the two of them have spoken for quite a while. Think, Ceri, think! Then the answer presents itself. One of Alex's neighbours, a young guy named Pete, steps into the street and he begins walking in the direction of the shops. I quickly start up the engine and park the other side of the small row of shops. I casually saunter inside and walk up and down the aisles several times, as if I'm looking for something. Suddenly I hear my name.

"Ceri! Hey, you're looking good. What are you doing in this part of town? You haven't moved?"

"Pete. Hi! No, I'm passing through."

"Not visiting Alex?" he asks.

"No, no, nothing like that. I'm on my way back from an event and I need a sugar lift. I haven't seen him in ages, I heard he's in a serious relationship these days." I reach for a big bar of chocolate as if I really don't care what the answer is.

"Well, if you count Harry as a relationship, then yes, I suppose his is." He laughs. "Are you, you know, are you seeing someone, because if you aren't…"

I can't believe he's hitting on me! My head is spinning, if anyone knows whether Alex is seeing anybody at the moment it would be Pete. He makes it his business to check out everything that happens in the building. I realise he's looking at me expectantly.

"Um. I'm sort of off men at the moment."

His eyes widen. I don't like the thought that crosses his mind.

"Really…" he replies, then I realise he thinks I've changed sides. I say a quick goodbye and head off to pay for the chocolate.

As I exit the shop I have a big smile plastered over my face. I open the wrapper on the bar of chocolate and pop a large piece into my mouth. I hear my name being called once more. This time its Alex's voice that carries through the air.

"Alex?"

"Ceri? What on earth are you doing here? And why are you watching my apartment?"

Panic sets in. I don't know what to say. Harry leaps forward, knocking the chocolate out of my hands and he's all over it before Alex or I can stop him.

"Don't you know chocolate is poisonous for dogs?" He scoops up Harry before he can finish off the last little pieces. He looks frantic.

"Jump in," I unlock the car and open the rear door. "There's a rug in the back if you want to wrap it around Harry. Where's the nearest vet?"

"Head towards the bridge, then hang left. Second on the right, you can't miss it."

Harry starts growling, and for such a small dog it's quite a vicious sound. A constant low rumbling.

"Is he okay?"

"How do I know? I've never been stupid enough to give him chocolate before. Only a tiny amount can be very dangerous for a dog his size. He's never growled before, so can you please just concentrate on getting us there in one piece as quickly as you can."

It's only a couple of miles, but the journey is agony. Please don't die little dog, or Alex will hate me forever.

I drop Alex at the door and he dashes into the building with Harry in his arms, still growling. I park the car and venture inside, taking a deep breath before I open the door.

The receptionist looks up. "I'm waiting for Harry," I mumble.

"Oh, yes, chocolate OD." It sounds funny and a small smile creeps over my face, but she gives me a withering look. I don't know anything about dogs, but even I know they aren't supposed to have chocolate. I have no idea why, though.

"I'm the driver," I offer, jangling my keys in front of her to prove it and her face relaxes.

"Your friend is very upset," she says.

"How dangerous is it?" I ask.

"It contains theobromine, which can cause cardiac arrhythmias, epileptic seizures, internal bleeding, heart attacks and eventually death. It depends on the quality of the chocolate, only a couple of ounces in a dog that size can be fatal. He's in safe hands, please take a seat."

Just when you think life can't throw anything else at you, there's always a surprise around the corner.

Thirty minutes later the internal door opens and Alex steps through. Harry isn't with him. He shakes the vet's hand and walks over to me. He runs a hand through his hair. "I need a drink. Harry's going to be fine, but they are keeping him overnight."

I hurry out the door after him.

"Alex, I'm so sorry, I don't really understand about the chocolate thing and dogs, but the receptionist said it causes poisoning."

"Yes. They gave Harry an injection and it made him sick. The vet seems to think the residual effects will go in twenty-four hours. Harry's a bit hyper at the moment and they will be watching him around the clock."

I'm mortified.

"Well?" he stands with his hands on his hip, empty leash swinging from his wrist. "Are you going to at least drive me back to my place?"

"Of course." I unlock the car and Alex settles into the passenger seat.

"I think you owe me an explanation." His voice is grim, and the rest of the journey is in total silence.

Chapter Nineteen – Coming Clean

Alex laughs, then he roars, and then tears begin leaking out of his eyes. He rolls around on the sofa as if he's in pain. All I can do is sit, watching him and grasping my car keys so tightly in my hand that little spots of blood begin to break through the pressure points.

He takes a few minutes to calm himself. It's hardly the reaction I expected after he dragged the full, sorry story out of me.

"You're really telling me that you've spend the last few days sitting in your car just watching me?"

"I had to know whether you were happy." I know it sounds pathetic, but there it is.

"Poor Harry has gone through all of this because you couldn't dial my number or send me an email, like anyone else would have done?"

"I rang you and there was no answer. I did send you an email, too."

"Okay, maybe I haven't been picking up my calls. But I've been away on business and the flight home was a long one. Where's the email? It's not in my inbox." He looks at me accusingly.

"Look in spam."

He stands up and walks through into the study. Two minutes later he shouts out "The answer is yes, I can forgive you, and of course I love you, idiot – even if you did try to poison my dog."

He reappears and before I know it we are kissing as if we've never been apart.

"There's no one else?" I ask.

"No, I decided that nothing could top what we had, so what was the point in kidding myself that I could settle for less? The thing about soul mates," he breathes softly into my ear, "is that it's forever."

Eighteen months later...

Chapter Twenty – Is There Such A Thing As Happy Ever After?

As I finish doing my hair, Alex appears in the doorway.

"I want to take you out for breakfast. Throw on something nice, I'm talking about the best joint in town." I have no idea who exactly he's trying to impersonate, but it makes me laugh.

"Is that Irish, Australian-American? Give me a clue."

"It was the Godfather actually, Marlon Brando at his best!" He flashes that cheeky grin at me and my heart melts, as if it's the first time we met all over again.

"Well, I'm thinking French toast, maple syrup and crispy bacon. Can you stretch to a Bloody Mary? I always think it's such a decadent think to have for breakfast! And why exactly are you spoiling me?"

He walks across to me and as I stand up, we hug. He lifts me in his arms and spins me around.

"Because you are you," is all he says.

There's something really wonderful about the crisp, morning air and a leisurely walk to a gourmet breakfast.

"Where are you taking me?" He tightens his grip on my hand and gives it an extra little squeeze.

"Lanbury's. I booked a table yesterday. I thought it would be a rather nice way to end one amazingly, unbelievable week."

As we wait for the traffic lights to change, Harry strains forward and Alex eases him back. We stand there smiling. Not necessarily at each other, but at life in general.

"Can we take Seb and…" before I can complete my sentence, Harry's collar breaks away from the lead and Alex suddenly lets go of my hand. It's so unexpected that it takes several seconds for it to register and for my gaze to follow them. One moment he's here, next to me and then…

Alex yells at Harry, frantically waving his arms as he careers towards the scared animal, who has stopped in the middle of the intersection. One moment Alex is running and the next he's in the air, hit sideways by a car that didn't see him. A woman scoops Harry up and cradles him in her arms. Everything has come to a halt and my legs automatically begin running, even though my mind cannot accept the scene I'm witnessing.

The driver is in a state of shock and someone is talking to her through the broken side window, urging her not to move. Where's Alex? He must be fine, I can't see him. As I run around to the other side of the car he's there, lying on the floor with his eyes closed. As if he's asleep. There's very little blood, but it's coming from the back of his head. I drape myself lightly around him, letting him feel the warmth of my body, as his soul hovers above him, waiting for his spirit guides to help him find his way back home.